Mills & Boon
Best Seller Romance

A chance to read and collect some of the best-loved novels from Mills & Boon— the world's largest publisher of romantic fiction.

Every month, four titles by favourite Mills & Boon authors will be re-published in the *Best Seller Romance* series.

A list of other titles in the *Best Seller Romance* series can be found at the end of this book.

Anne Hampson

THE REBEL BRIDE

MILLS & BOON LIMITED
LONDON · TORONTO

First published 1971
Australian copyright 1982
Philippine copyright 1982
This edition 1982

© Harlequin Enterprises B. V. 1971

ISBN 0 263 73851 5

Set in Linotype Baskerville 10 on 11pt
02–0482

Made and printed in Great Britain by
Richard Clay (The Chaucer Press) Ltd,
Bungay, Suffolk

CHAPTER ONE

FROM the verandah of her bedroom Judy looked over the narrow coastal plain to the lovely bay of Kyrenia. To the east the harbour was dominated by the castle, while in the distance, across a blue expanse of clear warm sea, rose the mountains of Turkey, snow-capped, and gleaming in the sun.

The lovely island of Cyprus had been Judy's home since she was five years old when, on the death of her parents within three months of each other, her maternal grandfather, a Greek Cypriot, had without hesitation accepted responsibility for her. He had given her love, a luxurious home and a good education. But he had brought her up in the way Cypriot girls were brought up, with a strictness amounting to severity and near imprisonment. However, when she was sixteen he had sent her to school in France; she had remained there for a year, and on her return two months ago he relaxed a little and she was allowed to go out on her own, visiting friends in Nicosia and on other parts of the island.

She turned into her bedroom, no longer interested in the scenic beauty outside. Picking up a comb, she tidied her hair and then, with a glance at the clock, she hurried downstairs. Her grandfather was sitting on the patio reading his newspaper and she watched him a moment in spite of the fact that she was catching a bus in less than a quarter of an hour. Wizened by a merciless sun, he looked much older than his sixty-two years. But there was a noble appearance about him which was emphasized by the firm jaw and mouth, the low forehead and fine dark eyes. His hair was jet-black still, his face burnt browner than an Arab's; he was slim and masculine, and very tall—far different from the average Cypriot, who was invariably stocky and overweight.

Christalis would be like him some day, she thought. Christalis to whom she was betrothed by her grandfather's choosing and design. The marriage had been arranged two years ago when Judy was fifteen and Chris twenty-six—arranged without Judy's ever having even set eyes on him, for she was sent into another room while the negotiations were going on. When at last she had seen him she had been struck with wonderment that he would consent to an arranged marriage. He was so distinguished and aristocratic, so haughty and self-confident, that she somehow thought he would have been more enlightened than to take part in one of the arranged marriages so common in Cyprus, and in Chris's own country of Greece. For Chris was not a Cypriot; he came from Athens but, like many wealthy ship-owners, he had a magnificent home on the island of Hydra, as well as a bungalow high above the mountain village of Karmi, in Cyprus. It was while staying there that he had seen Judy, when they had been attending church in Kyrenia. He had immediately offered for her and less than a week later the engagement party had taken place at the Corner Restaurant, one of the most magnificent and expensive places in Nicosia.

At the time of the engagement Judy had accepted that her grandfather's word was law and that she, like so many Cypriot girls, must face life with a man she did not love. But during the evening, as the party progressed, she began to feel a sudden fear of Chris, for he looked so formidable and aloof; and dwelling on the fact that two years must pass before the wedding was to take place, Judy subconsciously cherished the hope that something would happen to prevent its taking place at all.

But time was running out ... and to complicate matters Judy had met a young Englishman, Ronnie Tenant, one of the few foreigners allowed a work permit by the Cypriot government. Only technicians and people like Embassy officials were allowed to work on the island, for there were not enough jobs for the natives. Ronnie had been fortunate in landing a post with the television company in Nicosia, for he was an expert and, therefore, doing work that was extremely technical while at the same time teaching the young Cypriot who would eventually take his place. Judy had met him on the plane coming over from Athens where she had been visiting a friend and where Ronnie had changed planes on his flight from England.

They had been meeting in secret, but Judy knew a perpetual fear of discovery. In Cyprus girls did not go out with boys even if they were unattached ... and for an engaged girl to go out with someone else would be quite unthinkable. A dreadful scandal would follow discovery and the girl's name would be blackened for ever.

'Grandfather,' she said at last, moving towards him, 'I'm going to Nicosia. I want things for Manoula's wedding——'

'Manoula's wedding?' he frowned, lowering his newspaper. 'But you went into Nicosia twice last week. I thought you now had everything you need.'

She swallowed hard, her beautiful blue eyes fixed on her hands, which were clasped nervously in front of her.

'Not everything, Grandfather. I still want a sash for my dress and some—and some ribbons for my hair.' She glanced up. Was her grandfather looking at her

7

with suspicion, or was it merely her frightened imagination playing her tricks?

'I see. Well, you had better go, then.' He glanced at his watch. 'And you'll have to hurry if you're going to catch the convoy. What time does the bus go?'

'In ten minutes' time. I'll be back on the five-fifteen.'

'See that you are, Judy. You haven't forgotten your fiancé is coming to dinner this evening? He'll be here early, though, about six o'clock, he said in his letter.'

She nodded, and went for the bus. Chris coming. How many times had she seen him altogether? There was the day they became engaged, when she had been brought out of the lounge by her great-aunt, Astero, her grandfather's sister. Shyly and reluctantly she had entered the sitting-room and met the man who had offered for her and who had been accepted by her grandfather. He had looked at her without any sign of emotion—and there had not been even one kiss to seal the contract between them. The second time they had met was at the engagement party. Chris had given most of his time and attention to her grandfather—probably discussing the dowry, she thought—and the rest of his time was spent in chatting to his friends who had been invited to the party. But once or twice she had caught Chris glancing at her, and it was with the customary examination of her body, as if he were silently speculating on the degree of pleasure it would afford him when the time came for him to possess it. This was no more unusual than his indifference towards her, and Judy, having been brought up to accept such things, did not take offence or feel she was in any way being treated with disrespect. Nevertheless, she did blush, in much the same way a Cypriot girl would blush, and her fiancé's straight black brows were raised in a gesture of amusement.

The third time they met was at Margarita's wedding.

8

Chris happened to be over in Cyprus, taking a rest from business in his villa above Karmi, and he accepted the invitation to Margarita's wedding even though she was a total stranger to him, and so was her betrothed. But in Cyprus the whole village was invited to a wedding and it was traditional that if one received an invitation one must accept. On that occasion Chris had danced with Judy, and had talked with her for a little while, but the conversation was no more intimate than if they had been casual acquaintances who had met for the first time at the wedding.

And now Chris was coming again ... This time to arrange the wedding—no doubt about that. Judy ran as the bus was moving away and the driver stopped. They had been on their way only a few minutes when one of the passengers found he had no cigarettes; again the driver stopped, so that the man could go into a nearby shop and buy some. Within a short while they had joined the convoy; there was the usual checking by the Turkish officials. One of them boarded the bus and took the seat in front of Judy, smiling at her as he sat down. She smiled in response and they chatted for a space until the convoy began to move, snaking its way through the magnificent Kyrenia Range before reaching the arid, treeless Messaoria Plain in the centre of which was situated the beautiful capital of the island.

Three-quarters of an hour later she was hurrying to cover the distance from the bus to the gardens which now occupied the moat below the Venetian walls surrounding the old city of Nicosia. Down the steps she ran, to the café in the garden, where Ronnie was seated at a table right in the corner, under a swaying date palm. Over the weathered ochre wall close by, a bougainvillea tumbled down in a shower of purple bloom, gleaming in the sunshine.

9

'Darling, you made it!' Rising quickly, he held out a hand; Judy took it and held it and then put it to her cheek. 'I thought you weren't coming,' said Ronnie. 'I'll order and then we can talk. Sit down, sweetheart.' Clapping his hands for the waiter, he then ordered refreshments for them, frowning as she looked furtively about her.

'Ronnie ... Grandfather asked questions—oh, nothing serious, but I was frightened. I can't give the same excuse again.' Suddenly her eyes filled up. 'I don't think I can come again, Ronnie. And this evening Chris is dining with us; it's only so he can discuss our marriage; I'm sure of it.'

Ronnie's frown deepened.

'Judy, you must break this engagement——'

'Break it?' she cut in, her big eyes clouded with fear. 'I can't, Ronnie—no, that's not possible. An engagement's as binding as a marriage here, you must know that.'

'You're not one of these subjugated Cypriot girls! Your grandfather has no right to question you about your movements—much less has he the right to force you into marriage with someone you don't even know!' She was dumb, for this was not the response she had expected from Ronnie. And yet what did she expect? There was nothing he could do to help her. He had signed a two-year contract and could not leave the island until it expired. But she could not marry Chris, loving Ronnie as she did.

'What can we do?' she faltered. 'Ronnie, I'm so desolate at the idea of being married to Chris——'

'You can't be forced into it. All you have to do is break this engagement—flatly refuse to go on with the marriage. No one can force you. It's just that you lack courage,' he added. 'And that's because you've been brought up here and you feel bound by the customs—

and they are only customs, you know, Judy. There's no law to say you must obey your grandfather in this.'

Quite true, she admitted, but custom was strong, just as it had been strong in England many years ago. In medieval times the 'laws' of the Manor were in reality only feudal customs, but no one ever thought of disregarding them.

'I can't, Ronnie,' she faltered. 'Oh, help me—take me away somewhere!'

'Somewhere? On a small island like this? Where could you hide?—and in any case you've just said you can't break the engagement.'

She looked at him, her eyes brimming. Did he love her, as he had said he did the last time they met?

'I can't break the engagement if I have to face them—my grandfather and Chris, I mean—but I could run away——' She stopped, because he was frowning heavily, but as he saw her expression his face cleared and he smiled at her. Grasping at this slight sign of encouragement, she went on to suggest, tentatively, that Ronnie might be able to find her an apartment in Nicosia where she could live in hiding until his contract expired, and then they could go to England together and be married. But Ronnie was frowning again, and shaking his head.

'You're under age,' he reminded her. 'And your grandfather is your legal guardian, after all. I should be in dreadful trouble were I to assist you to leave his care. No, Judy, there's only one solution; you must break the engagement. Then you can tell your grandfather you've met someone else and I can come and talk to him. If he'll accept me as your young man, and give his consent, we can be married here.'

'He won't let me break the engagement,' she cried, her heart like a leaden weight inside her. 'I dare not mention it.' She fell silent as the waiter appeared with their drinks, and then she spoke again. 'He would want a reason.'

'Simply say you don't love this man.'

'That's not a good enough reason. People here don't marry for love. Besides, Grandfather would want to know why I hadn't objected before.'

He looked at her.

'You'd have gone into it willingly, and meekly, if you hadn't met me?'

She nodded.

'It's customary—and I was resigned.'

'Because you've been brought up to consider the male as all-important, whose wishes must be obeyed. This wouldn't have happened had you been brought up in England.'

'But I haven't been brought up in England and therefore I can't bring myself to disobey my grandfather.' A Cypriot girl would not even allow such a thought to enter her head. Her parents or guardian were held in supreme reverence; their word was law in everything. Judy felt like a Cypriot girl, which was natural, seeing that she had only the vaguest memory of her life in England before her parents were so tragically killed.

'You say you can't break this engagement without giving a reason,' Ronnie was saying. 'Then tell your grandfather the truth—that you've met me.'

She stared at him, appalled at that idea.

'I dare not,' she quivered. 'I dare not tell him I've been seeing you secretly!'

Ronnie sighed impatiently, and did not speak immediately. Judy watched him, and her heart ached because she could not be with him always, because she could not take him to her grandfather and introduce him as her young man—as they did in France, and in England. Yes, she'd learned a lot during that year in

France—and she had seen English films and seen how she would have lived had not fate decreed that she should be brought up in this island where parental control remained so strong that even the young men were completely subdued. True, they were beginning to object, and when interviewed on television they expressed these objections quite strongly, but in the East change is slow and Judy felt it would be many years yet before the girls and boys of Cyprus were free to go about together before marriage and, therefore, able to find the one they could love.

'If you won't break the engagement,' said Ronnie at last, 'there's nothing we can do.'

'Nothing?' Her eyes filled up and she flicked away the tears with her fingers. 'But, Ronnie—if you love me...?'

'I love you—haven't I said that, Judy?' He made a gesture with his hands. 'Darling, what can I do to help you if you won't help yourself?'

'I suppose,' she whispered after a pause, 'I'm being quite unreasonable.'

He eyed her perceptively.

'In expecting me to do something?'

She swallowed hard.

'If—if p-people really love each other, they try t-to find a way.' Words were difficult because to Judy it seemed as if Ronnie had not been impressed very much by what she had said up till now. She knew from novels she read and films she had seen that trials often came the way of lovers, but they always strove to find a way out and of being happy together in the end.

'You consider I'm not trying hard enough and so I don't really love you, is that it?' She could not answer because he was looking so accusingly at her. His blue eyes were narrowed, his brow creased beneath the lock of fair hair which had fallen on to it.

'I could say the same about you, Judy,' he said reprovingly. 'The whole solution is in your hands. No one can make you marry this Chris ... and if you're so weak-willed that you do go through with it, you'll regret it till the end of your days.'

Ronnie's words were with her as she sat at the table that evening with her grandfather and her fiancé. They were true, of course. If she did marry Chris she would regret it till the end of her days, but how was she to get out of it? Several times, while they were sitting on the patio, waiting for the servant to announce dinner, she had opened her mouth to tell them she did not want to marry Chris, but the words not only stuck in her throat; they actually choked her. It was so strange to know that had she been brought up in England, with her parents, she would now be a very modern miss with stacks of self-confidence and a will of her own which no one would be able to oppose. But she was now a little Cypriot girl, timid and meek and so afraid of these two men that she could not speak her mind, even though by her silence she was sentencing herself to a life of subjugation.

Chris was speaking to her grandfather and as always when men were in conversation Judy followed the normal pattern and remained silent, listening, and yet thinking all the time of Ronnie and the kiss he had given her when they parted. They had gone on to the car park, and sat in his car, waiting an unconscionable length of time before the park was deserted and Ronnie could take her in his arms. And she did not really enjoy his kiss because she was looking over his shoulder in case someone should come on the car park and see them. That was the trouble with a small island; you couldn't do anything without someone seeing you, and as everyone seemed to know everyone else gossip spread widely and swiftly. She looked across at Chris, sitting

14

opposite to her. If he should ever learn that she had kissed someone else.... Her heart actually jumped at the thought and in her nervousness her knife clattered against her plate. Her fiancé's brows rose questioningly and she flushed. He smiled then, clearly amused. Funny, she thought, but he seemed so very Westernized ... and yet he had offered for her in the manner of his people, and was quite willing to take part in an arranged marriage. Judy did not know why, but right from the first he had struck her as a man who, if he married at all, it would be for love.

'I suppose I'm a romantic,' she said to herself. And added, 'But Lefki is too, because she has been to school in France, and she looks at the English films on television. I think I will go and see her tomorrow, because she had never seen Paul till the engagement, and yet she's deliriously happy with him.'

'Judy——' Her musings were brought to an abrupt halt by the voice of her grandfather. 'You're not eating, my dear. Come, what are you thinking about? Your forthcoming marriage?' he added, a twinkle in his eye. She frowned. Why did they always pretend it was all so romantic? For they did—even if some poor girl was dragging herself to church with tears in her eyes and a heart that was breaking the whole village pretended the couple were in love.

'No, I'm not thinking of my marriage,' she returned without any effort at tact, and again her fiancé's brows rose a fraction.

'You're not exactly enamoured with the prospect,' he commented drily.

She looked at him, her eyes clouded. What would he say if she told him she was in love with someone else?

'I think I'm a little young for marriage,' she returned in quiet tones.

'You're seventeen and a half,' put in her grandfather. 'That is a nice ripe age. Girls are usually ready by then.'

Ready ... ripe. She felt a little sick. Ronnie would never use such expressions; he had more delicacy, but then sex was the beginning and end of marriage here. Rarely did one see a love match made, and even on the rare occasion when the couple did fall in love—which was in any case usually after marriage—the man still retained his own interests which were completely alien from those of his wife.

'If we could postpone it for another year,' began Judy, looking at Chris and wondering what would be the result should she get him on his own and plead with him. But her grandfather would not allow her to be alone with him—— Her meditations ceased abruptly. If Chris wanted to be alone with her she felt quite sure nothing would stop him. So firm and taut that chin, and those lines from nose to mouth ... they seemed to spell out the word 'domination'. And the arrogant superiority of him! He was even more distinguished than her grandfather, she thought, and even more self-possessed and confident. Perhaps riches made one arrogant and superior like that, or perhaps it was merely his magnificent physique and height that made him so proud and haughty. With her, though, he adopted an air of rather bored tolerance; he seemed quiet and unemotional, but once or twice this evening he had regarded her with a sort of amused indulgence, almost as if he considered her a child.

'Another year,' her grandfather was saying. 'No, my dear, Chris here has come to discuss the marriage and we have decided it shall be next month——'

'Next month!' She stared at him, aghast. 'No, Grandfather, not so soon as that!'

Chris flicked her a glance.

'Diplomacy doesn't appear to be one of your virtues,

16

my dear,' he remarked a little crisply. 'Why not next month?'

'It's t-too soon,' she faltered. She thought: it's like Christmas; you wait and wait and then suddenly it's upon you. 'I couldn't be ready.'

'Nonsense; you have about twenty maids of honour to do everything for you.' Her grandfather seemed a trifle embarrassed, and he gave her a stern and censorious glance. 'I must apologize for Judy,' he then said to Chris. 'Please make allowances—her father was English and she never forgets that.'

'She has been brought up to know her place, though,' returned Chris. 'At least I hope she has. I'm not expecting to have to deal with a rebellious wife.'

'No, oh, certainly not,' hurriedly put in the old man. 'Judy is most meek and obedient. She will not give you the slightest trouble.'

A short while later Judy was sent to bed, while her grandfather and her fiancé went into the sitting-room to discuss the wedding.

Lefki, Judy's married friend, lived in a luxury flat on the outskirts of Nicosia. She was twenty-one and had been married for four years; she had three little girls, but her husband employed a nanny for them, and in addition he had a maid living at the flat and a daily woman to come in and clean. Whenever Judy visited Lefki she was either reclining on the couch, looking elegant and fresh, or she was sitting at a table working on her most exquisite embroidery. She went to the hairdressers often and her black hair had been bleached and then dyed an attractive shade of auburn. Her nails were always immaculate, her clothes models of perfection. Twice a year her husband took her to London and she would return literally loaded with Georgian silver. This was elegantly displayed about the flat, mainly in cabinets in the massive sitting-room. The carpet had come from Persia, the furniture from France.

A uniformed maid opened the door, smiling instantly on seeing who it was.

'Miss Benson—how nice to see you! Mrs. Mavritis is in the sitting-room. She said you had rung earlier and she's been looking forward to seeing you.'

'Judy...' Lefki held out both her hands. 'I've been wondering when you'd come. But how well you look! I think you grow more beautiful every day, while I——' She shook her head in mock dejection. 'I am now past my prime.'

Judy laughed and sat down, looking round.

'You've been to London again since last I was here.'

'Do you like my trays, and my candlesticks? I spent three thousand pounds!'

'Three——?' Judy stared incredulously. 'No, Lefki, you surely couldn't have?'

'Certainly I did.' Lefki shrugged. 'Paul has plenty. Why shouldn't I spend money? He likes to give it me and I like to spend it, so we have a wonderful arrangement.' She sat down opposite to Judy and rang a little silver bell. 'Kyria, will you make some tea, please?' she said when the maid appeared.

Lefki and Judy chatted about everyday things until the tea came, then Lefki, the cool and elegant hostess, poured the tea from a silver pot and handed Judy hers, smiling affectionately at her as she did so.

'How long have you been home now?' she asked after a while.

'Almost three months.' A small silence and then, with a sort of frightened urgency, 'Tell me—truthfully —are you happy with Paul? Oh, I know you've said many times that you are, but is it only the money you like, or do you ... love Paul, really love him, I mean?'

'But of course I love Paul, and he loves me.' Lefki's eyes opened wide. 'Why do you ask? I've always said we're deliriously happy.' And she certainly looked happy; her eyes were shining and there was a most contented expression on her face. 'I don't know why you should suddenly ask me this question, Judy.'

Judy glanced down at her hands and said quietly,

'Your marriage was arranged, as is usual, but I never asked you how long you'd known Paul before you married him?'

'Two months,' supplied Lefki, still puzzled. 'As you know, I'd never seen him until we were engaged, but he'd seen me. He liked me and his parents came to see my mother. I had just come home from school in France and Mother thought it was time I was married because I was seventeen. I wanted to be married, and I wanted a rich man. Paul was not only rich but handsome, and believe me I wouldn't have waited that long, only we got engaged at the end of November and, as you know, in Cyprus it's impossible to get married then.'

Judy nodded. No marriages took place during the forty days before Christmas; this was custom because during that time people's minds were supposed to be devoutly concerned with the festival of the birth of Christ.

'During that two months did you see each other often?'

'Every night. Mother was there, though.'

'Every night...?' Judy spoke musingly, almost to herself.

'You've known Chris much longer, haven't you? Is it about two years since you became engaged?'

'Yes, it's just over two years.' She put her cup down on her saucer and looked straight at Lefki. 'I don't know him, though, and I'm—I'm frightened.' Should she confide in Lefki? She might tell Paul, and Paul might tell his cousin. His cousin knew several people in Karmi—and Chris was staying at his house just higher up the mountain.

'Frightened? What about?'

'I don't want to be married, Lefki!'

'But how silly. Marriage is wonderful.'

'For you, but you're lucky. In fact, you're the only one I know who's happy. Poor Manoula was crying bitterly last night. She doesn't want to marry Panos.'

'Well, who would want to marry Panos?' returned Lefki with a shudder. 'Your Chris isn't like that; he's wonderful—almost as good-looking as my Paul.'

All unknowing, Judy lifted her chin.

'He's even better-looking than Paul, and he's much taller.'

'I don't agree—oh, about the height, yes, but to me Paul's the handsomest man I've ever seen.'

'When did you see Chris?' asked Judy, puckering her brow in thought.

'At Margarita's wedding, don't you remember?'

Judy's face cleared.

'Of course. You said I was lucky.' Judy frowned as she said that, and Lefki noticed.

'What's wrong, Judy?' she inquired, eyeing her curiously. 'It's not usual for a girl to want to change her mind.'

'I'm not a Cypriot, Lefki. In England couples fall in love and then get married.'

'You've lived as a Cypriot,' Lefki reminded her matter-of-factly, 'and your grandfather will expect you to obey him. You'll probably fall in love after you're married—like Paul and me.' Judy said nothing; she was thinking of Ronnie and her heart was heavy. Somehow she knew for sure that nothing could save her from Chris, and so she must spend the rest of her life loving someone else ... 'I should think you would be bound to fall in love with Chris, he's so handsome and rich. And he'll be sure to fall in love with you, because you're very beautiful, Judy.'

'I'm only ordinary,' Judy began, her face colouring at her friend's flattery. Lefki interrupted her before she could continue.

'You're far from ordinary. Just look at your hair, so soft and long and golden. I pay three pounds a week to my hairdresser and can't get mine like that.'

'You wouldn't want it so fair as mine,' put in Judy reasonably. 'It wouldn't suit your skin. I think you have your hair done beautifully.'

'Perhaps—but I have to watch the black roots,' laughed the older girl. 'However, we weren't talking about my assets, but yours. Those eyes are enough to cause any man's heart to quicken, and your mouth is just the sort men like to kiss, wide and full——'

'Lefki,' interrupted Judy, forced to laugh in spite of her dejection, 'do stop this nonsense!'

'All right. But I still think he'll fall in love with you, once you're married,' she said, and Judy became thoughtful.

Did she want him to fall in love with her? Since meeting Ronnie she had often felt she hated Chris, and the thought of either of them falling in love with one another had never even entered her mind.

'Tell me about France?' urged Judy after a small silence. 'You were in Paris a fortnight ago—oh, and thanks for the card. It brought back memories. I was happy at school.' Happy and carefree, learning how people of the West lived.

Lefki was eager to relate all that had happened on her visit to Paris with her husband; they had spent a fortune from all accounts, and Judy again wondered if it were only the money that made her friend happy.

But surely money alone could not bring that glow to her face.

'I had some fun with a taxi-driver,' Lefki was saying. 'And Paul became very cross with me over it. You see, he took us a long way round, thinking we didn't know, so I told him off——'

'*You* told him off? Didn't Paul say anything?'

'No, he said we should have paid and said nothing, but I was angry at the idea of being made a fool of. Well, this taxi-driver began to curse me, thinking I wouldn't be able to retaliate—just having learned the nice, drawing-room sort of French. However, what he didn't know was that my nanny is half French and I've made her teach me all the *other* words——'

'You didn't!' Judy interrupted, shocked. Lefki looked far too elegant and ladylike to use the words, anyway.

'I did, because it's no use learning half a language. You should have seen that taxi-driver's face——' Lefki broke off, throwing back her head and laughing heartily. 'He just stood there, dumbstruck, while I let him have it. Then he looked at me in a sort of admiring way and asked me where I'd learned it all. But Paul was furious with me, and wouldn't speak to me for two whole hours. But then I said if he was going to sulk like that I was getting the next plane home. That brought him round!'

Judy looked curiously at her. There was no doubt at all that Lefki knew exactly how to handle her husband. There was no subjugation here, nothing different, in fact, from a marriage one would expect to see in England. How had Lefki done it? But there was only one answer. Paul was in love with her. Yes, Judy no longer had any doubts about her friend's marriage. It was perfect, because they had been lucky enough to have fallen in love with one another after marriage.

'I must be going,' said Judy reluctantly on glancing at the clock. 'Chris comes to dinner every evening now and I mustn't be late. I have to dress up for him, Grandfather says.'

'Don't you like dressing up for him?'

'Not really. I keep thinking that if he suddenly decides he doesn't like me he might break the engagement.'

'Break——?' Lefki stared at her in astonishment. 'You know very well that'll never happen.'

Judy stood up, sighing.

'Yes, I know. I suppose I'm just hoping for a miracle.'

'Is it really as bad as that?' Lefki rose from her chair and stood facing her friend. 'It'll be all right, Judy, I know it will. When is the wedding?—or haven't you fixed it yet?'

'We haven't fixed the date, but Grandfather says it has to be next month.'

'Well, you've waited two years, and that's a long while.'

'I was only fifteen, Lefki,' Judy reminded her with some indignation.

'You were, yes, of course. But poor Chris. He's had to wait all this time for you to grow up. How old is he?'

'Twenty-eight.'

'He must have liked you to offer when you were only fifteen. He knew he'd have to wait some considerable time for you.'

He must have liked her ... Judy thought about that as she rode home on the bus. Desired her, more like, and with a Greek desire once aroused is so strong that he would wait a good deal longer than two years for his desire to be fulfilled.

CHAPTER TWO

It was in the cool of a summer evning, when they were sitting on the verandah, that her grandfather put the question. Over dinner, which this time they had taken alone, Chris having made a previous arrangement to dine out with friends, the old man had been silent, merely glancing at Judy now and then from under lowered brows. She knew something was wrong, but she was totally unprepared for what he had to say.

'Who is this man you've been meeting, Judy?'

She jumped, and her heart seemed to leap right up into her throat.

'M-man?'

'Don't prevaricate! It's all over Kyrenia that you've a boy-friend. You don't need me to tell you that your good name's ruined, that you've brought the direst disgrace on me and all my family. Who is he? Answer me at once!'

Her face was white; a terrible shudder passed through her. But in spite of her fear she experienced a tinge of relief. Her guilty secret was a burden which weighed her down and she was almost glad to be sharing it with someone as she said, though in a low and trembling voice,

'He's English, Grandfather, and—we love each other.'

He looked at her and she saw the grey lines about his mouth. She loved him dearly and the knowledge that he suffered hurt her exceedingly. Only now did she stop to think how deep his hurt would have gone had she run away and found a hiding-place in Nicosia as she would have done, had Ronnie been willing to help her.

'Where did you meet him?' he asked, pain and censure in his voice.

'On the plane—when I was coming home from that visit to Luciana in Athens.'

'So this is what happens when you're allowed a little freedom. This I did allow only because your father was English and I felt it was unfair, as you got older, to treat you entirely as a Cypriot.' He shook his head sadly. 'I should have known better, should have kept you under my eye. You realize, of course, that Chris will not marry you if this comes to his ears.'

Hope leapt; it was revealed in her eyes.

'I want to marry Ronnie, Grandfather. Please—please let me! I don't want to hurt you, but since I met Ronnie I've been so unhappy at the idea of marrying Chris.'

For a while the old man was silent, and Judy herself dared not speak while he was thus occupied in thought. Was he considering her plea? He loved her, she knew, and he would be greatly troubled were he to think she was unhappy. Perhaps, she thought breathlessly, she should have told him before, been frank with him and asked him to meet Ronnie.

Time passed; the fleeting twilight shades of gold and orange and rust melted into the deep purple of night. Stars appeared, hanging like diamonds suspended beneath a canopy of softest tulle. A wisp of cloud here and there, a floating moon, the calm dark sea, and carried on the breeze the scent of roses and jasmine. Sheep bells on the mountainside, a distant bray of a donkey.... This was Cyprus, island in the sun.

'This man,' said her grandfather at last, 'this Ronnie —he loves you, you say?'

'Yes.' Breathless again, she was—and wildly hopeful.
'And I love him.'

'You've known each other about nine weeks.'

She nodded, afraid to own that she knew Ronnie far
better than she knew Chris, to whom she had been
engaged for over two years.

'How often have you been seeing him?'

The question she dreaded, but she could not lie to
her grandfather and she was forced to confess to seeing
Ronnie every time she went to Nicosia.

'It's sometimes twice a week,' she added reluctantly,
watching for any change in his expression that would
tell her he was angry. But he remained oddly sad,
although his mouth was tight.

'Your—er—shopping, then, was merely an excuse.'
He looked straight at her and she lowered her head in
contrition. 'That you could deceive me like this——'
He shook his head as if quite unable to believe it.
'What has come over you, child, that you could act
with such disregard for my feelings and my authority?'

'I'm sorry,' she said, tears on her lashes. 'I wouldn't
hurt you, Grandfather, nor would I disregard your
authority, but...'.

'Yes?' he queried as she tailed off. 'But what?'

She raised her head, and he saw the sparkle of tears
in her lovely blue eyes. His own eyes shadowed as he
awaited her reply.

'It was love,' she said simply.

The old man gave a deep sigh.

'This young man knows you're betrothed?'

'Yes, Grandfather, he knows.'

'Do you consider it honourable of him to meet you
when he knows you belong to someone else?'

'Belong?' She frowned at the word. Yet most Cypriot
girls were possessions of their husbands. Judy's
thoughts flashed to Lefki, who had learned so much

26

from her year in France and from her frequent visits to England. Lefki was no possession, but a wife and an equal. 'We fell in love. No one can help that.' She met his gaze. 'Grandfather, will you let me bring Ronnie to see you?'

'You're betrothed, Judy,' was the sharp response. 'Chris is expecting to be married next month.'

Very slowly Judy was gaining confidence. Could it be the result of her visit to Lefki? she wondered.

'Ronnie says the engagement isn't binding, because —because I had no choice but to accept the man you had chosen for me.' Despite her slowly emerging courage she could not meet his eyes as she spoke those words.

'Not binding?' her grandfather suddenly snapped. 'Obviously the man has no idea what he's talking about! I should have thought you'd have corrected him.' He stopped and waited for her to lift her head, then gave her a stern and censorious look. 'You made no objection at the time of the engagement. Why not?'

'I hadn't met Ronnie. I accepted Chris because you had chosen him for me, and—and I felt I must obey you.'

He scowled at her.

'You were quite happy with my choice,' he began, when she interrupted him.

'Not happy, Grandfather, but resigned.'

'Well, you're engaged to Chris and there's nothing we can do about it——'

'You would, if you could?' she cut in eagerly.

'I hate to see you unhappy, child,' he admitted, his glance softening. 'Nevertheless, I am not in a position to make any changes at this stage. You know full well that the engagement's binding—so much so that in some villages it's really the marriage itself. You had the usual church service, just like anyone else, and as I've said there's nothing we can do at this stage.'

She bit her lip. Hope had soared for a moment, only to be dashed again. The engagement was binding and in those villages to which her grandfather referred, the engaged couple would immediately live together at the house of the bride's parents. And often the first child would be born before the marriage proper took place. There was nothing wrong in this arrangement because it was custom—but of course it applied only to a few villages, and Cypriots in general did not like to talk about it. Nevertheless, it demonstrated the strength and importance of the engagement. In all her years in Cyprus Judy had never heard of one being broken.

And yet she persevered, for so much was at stake—her whole life's happiness, in fact.

'If you would speak to Chris about Ronnie——'

'Speak to Chris! On the contrary, I must do my best to keep it from him——'

'But you said he won't want to marry me if he finds out. Please, Grandfather, help me! If Chris doesn't want me and I don't want him then surely we can break the engagement.'

But the old man was shaking his head.

'The disgrace is great enough already. We must contrive to get you married before he discovers what you've been up to—although I don't know how that will be possible, for it's more than likely that he knows already.'

And it so happened that he did. His face was a dark mask of fury when, the following evening, he came to dine with Judy and her grandfather. A swift glance passed between them as they noted Chris's expression and Judy was so terrified that she instantly made for the door, intent on escaping—for the time being, at any rate. But the voice of her fiancé, reaching her like the crack of a whip, brought her round to face him, her cheeks on fire.

'Judy! Come here!' She could not move and he pointed to a spot on the carpet in front of him. 'I said come here.' Soft the voice all of a sudden, but darkly imperious and commanding. Slowly, reluctantly, she obeyed, stopping a little way from the place he had indicated, and throwing her grandfather a desperate pleading glance. 'What is this I hear about your disgraceful conduct? Explain, if you please!'

She swallowed, but fear blocked her throat. Again she sent a pleading glance in her grandfather's direction. He came to her rescue, speaking for her.

'Judy's met an Englishman, Chris,' he informed him without preamble. 'She says they're in love and she wants to break her engagement to you.'

Judy held her breath. She had not expected her grandfather to be so obliging or so helpful. Would Chris also be obliging? she wondered, searching his face but soon dropping her eyes under the dark fury and contempt she saw there.

'I gathered she'd met an Englishman,' returned Chris gratingly. 'Her disgraceful escapades are the talk of Kyrenia—and every village for miles around! Do you realize,' he said, turning to look at Judy, 'that no one now believes you to be chaste?'

Miserably she nodded. 'She's had a boy-friend' people would say with a sort of brushing together of their hands—a gesture indicative of contempt and 'casting off' as it were. 'No good!' And on the very rare occasion that such an occurrence did take place, the girl concerned was scorned by everyone and her chances of marriage were nil.

'I—we only met,' faltered Judy at last, 'in a café in Nicosia—in—in the gardens. . . .'

If only she had the courage of Lefki. Why should she

keep on thinking of her friend? Perhaps it was because Lefki had been to school in France, just as Judy had ... and Lefki had learned to stick up for herself. Why can't I stick up for myself? Judy wondered, but even as she looked up at her fiancé's angry countenance deep terror assailed her again.

'How long have you been meeting in this café?' he demanded.

'Nine w-weeks.'

His face went taut, and white lines of wrath crept up under the tan. He looked ready to murder her, she thought, and took an involuntary step towards her grandfather. Her move was prevented, however, by the grip of a vice on her wrist. Viciously she was twisted round again, brought facing Chris, and her chin was jerked up by the pressure of a hand underneath it. Judy's legs felt so weak she could have dropped. In the happy sheltered environment provided by her grandfather fear had never been known to her, but she was now so frightened that her senses reeled. Chris was so big and tall above her, so overpowering and masterful ... and so very, very angry. And yet she really had nothing to fear because once over these next few moments she would be free. Chris would not want to marry her now. She should be glad that the truth was out, even though there would be the dreadful disgrace to endure. People would look the other way; young men would leer, and rake her body with their eyes—imagining things....

'Nine weeks!' rasped Chris, glowering at her before turning his attention to her grandfather. 'You ... have you no control over her?'

'I'm sorry, Chris, terribly sorry. Judy has deceived me just as she's deceived you. She owned to having kept company with this man when I tackled her earlier today.' He spread his hands. 'Because of her English nationality I've allowed her a little freedom, but she's abused it. I realize I should have been firmer, but the damage is done now. However, perhaps it's not as bad as it seems. You don't want her, obviously, and as she wants this young Englishman——'

'What do you mean, I don't want her?' Releasing her chin but not her wrist, Chris put the question slowly and quietly to her grandfather. 'Judy and I are engaged.'

Judy gave a little gasp; her grandfather stared at Chris in disbelief.

'You still want to marry her?' he exclaimed. 'Despite the scandal!'

'I still want to marry her.' The grip on her wrist slackened. 'Despite the scandal,' he added, although Judy heard the soft gritting of his teeth and knew that the quietness with which he spoke was only a cover for his fury and disgust.

Her body sagged. Hope, it seemed, was at last quite dead.

'But you've just said that no one now believes her to be chaste.' So her grandfather was actually trying, she concluded, but her hopes could not be re-born. Chris's expression told her all she needed to know.

'Judy and I shall be living in Greece,' he said shortly.

A most odd expression settled on the old man's face as he watched Chris. He said slowly,

'You, apparently, believe that Judy has done no real wrong?'

Chris looked down at his fiancée, noting the dullness of her eyes and the droop of hopelessness about her mouth.

'I'm quite sure she's done no real wrong, otherwise I shouldn't be marrying her.' He let go of her wrist; she glanced down at it and saw the vivid red mark he had made.

'Grandfather...' She looked beseechingly at him, but he shook his head.

'Let's have no more argument,' he almost snapped. 'I've given my consent to your marriage; you're engaged to Chris——'

'But I love Ronnie!' The cry came involuntarily and Chris's dark eyes glinted.

'You'll forget all about this Englishman, understand?'

Helplessly she looked from one to the other. She was trapped, just as all Cypriot girls were trapped. She had tried to tell herself she was not one of them, because her father was English, and her nationality British, but she was one of them, in reality, because she must conform to the customs of Cyprus, must obey her grandfather, and bow to the will of her fiancé.

It was to be a fashionable wedding, at the church in Nicosia, and the reception was to be held at the Hilton. Invitations were sent out by the hundred; presents poured in. Judy telephoned Ronnie, pleading with him to help her even while fully aware that she was asking the impossible. He, as a foreigner, dared not take her from her legal guardian. But he was just as unhappy as she, especially as they could not even see one another, Judy being guarded by her grandfather who no doubt feared she would attempt to run away.

'You needn't go through with the marriage,' Ronnie said over and over again. 'No one can force you to do so.'

But she hadn't the courage to fight. Her grandfather she could have persuaded eventually, she thought, but Chris had said emphatically that he would not release her from the engagement.

And so Judy was married to a man she did not love—a beautiful bride at whose appearance gasps of admiration were uttered from all sides of the church. The bearded priest looked enviously at her husband, so tall and distinguished as he stood at her side. There were photographs to be taken as they came out; there was the brilliant reception, the laughter, the pretence. Through it all Judy felt numbed, as if her heart were a stone. Chris too did not betray even a hint of emotion. What a sham! Judy gazed down the table and her eyes caught those of her friend. Paul was beside her, handing her things, smiling at her.... Their wedding had been as splendid as this, she remembered, although at that time Judy and Lefki were not close friends and Judy had been invited merely because Lefki's great-aunt was related to Judy's grandfather by marriage. Lefki had wanted to be married, so although she and Paul did not fall in love until afterwards, Lefki would not be feeling like this—dead inside and pining her heart out for someone else.

Lefki winked, but Judy did not smile. She had wanted to visit Lefki again, but from the moment of discovery she had not been allowed out on her own for one single moment.

'My child, do try to look a little more cheerful,' ordered her husband, his mouth close to her ear. 'Anyone would think it was a funeral you were attending.'

She flushed and her nerves went tight. She looked at Lefki again, Lefki who had somehow managed to shed the chains of bondage and to become an equal with her husband....

'How did you do it?' Judy asked the question much later when she found an opportunity of speaking to her friend alone. The conversation had been veered into these channels by Judy who, driven by some vague force she could not understand, wanted to know more about Lefki's personality and the strength of which she was endowed that had made it possible for her to reach, and hold, this position of equality with her husband.

'It's the way you start,' laughed the Cypriot girl. 'If you begin by being timid and allowing yourself to be downtrodden, then you're lost immediately. Men are all puffed up with a sense of their own superiority and women are resigned to being subjugated—in this part of the world, at least. Well, I learned a lot when I was in France, and during my stay there I made friends with English girls and visited their homes. No being mastered for me, I said to myself when I saw how things were with the women of the West. Oh, I did appear to be meek and tractable before the wedding because I did not want Paul to guess what I was about. Once we were married, however, I began to train him in the way I wanted him to develop. And now we're the happiest couple in Cyprus!'

Judy still had not formed a clear picture of what Lefki had done and she said,

'Do you mean that whenever Paul told you to do something you deliberately went against his wishes?'

'If I didn't want to do what he asked, yes. I just disobeyed him.'

'But ...' Judy tailed off as her eyes strayed to Chris. He was standing, hands in his pockets, talking and laughing with a small crowd of young men. He towered above them and Judy noted his jaw and mouth. Would Lefki have dared disobey a man like Chris? Judy wondered, looking round for Paul. There he was, by the bar, handsome and strong, and certainly possessing a commanding personality. 'Perhaps you succeeded because he was in love with you. You might not have done so otherwise.'

'He wasn't in love with me right away. But even had he never loved me I'd still have had a good try.' She looked sideways at Judy and laughed. 'What are you

34

up to? Are you intending to follow my example?'

Judy fell silent. Why had she asked these questions of her friend?

'When you disobeyed him—what was his reaction?'

'He was quite astounded at first, naturally, because I'd led him to believe I was a meek and mild little thing. Then he tried to master me and we did have some dreadful rows,' she admitted with a grimace. 'But I held firm and in the end he became so fed up he capitulated.'

'And now you're—well, I suppose you're the boss, really?'

To her surprise Lefki shook her head vigorously.

'Far from it. I know just how far to go with Paul, and I don't proceed one step farther.' She actually gave a little shiver. 'He *is* masterful, and as I've said I know how far to go. He tolerates a lot, but then he suddenly won't tolerate any more and it is then that I prudently cease to fight.'

Judy frowned.

'How do you know when to stop?'

'I know my husband.' Lefki looked curiously at her, her big eyes alight with amusement. 'You're picking my brains, Judy,' she accused.

'No, I'm not. But I am endeavouring to learn something from you about—about ... She tailed off, scarcely able to frame her words and Lefki finished for her,

'About man-management?' Elegant hands were spread nonchalantly as Lefki's glance searched for her husband. 'It really isn't anything one can learn, Judy. It just comes. You've been in France, and you know what it's like in England. You surely kept your eyes open?'

'Yes, of course I did, but Chris—he's different.'

'Different?' Lefki raised her eyebrows. 'In some ways, perhaps, but all men are basically the same. Lie down and they'll trample on you; stand up to them and they'll usually see eye to eye simply because it's less wearing than being for ever in a tussle with you.'

'Does it always work?'

'Not always. For example, Kyria's husband beats her. She often comes in with her eyes all red from weeping. That makes me angry because she can't get on with her work and I have to help her.'

'Her husband beats her...' Again Judy sought out her own husband; he seemed aware of her scrutiny, for he turned and stared at her, questioningly but not with any particular sign of emotion. Judy flushed and looked away. 'So it doesn't always work.'

'That's what I've just said.' And then Lefki added, 'Of course, there's no affection at all between Kyria and her husband, whereas Paul and I love one another.'

'So it only works if your husband is in love with you? I did suggest that a short while back,' Judy reminded her friend.

'I think it would work better if your husband loves you,' admitted Lefki, and then she said, a twinkle in her eye, 'Do you remember I said Chris would fall in love with you, once you were married?' Judy shook her head and frowned but Lefki went on, 'He will, just you mark my words ... and then you'll be able to twist him right round your little finger——'

'Not Chris! No, it would be quite impossible! Besides, he'll never fall in love with me—and I don't want him to.'

Lefki's eyes flickered strangely.

'You wouldn't be in love with someone else, would you?' she softly inquired, and Judy looked up, startled.

'You've heard the rumour?'

'Everyone has,' came the frank reply. But then Lefki passed that off as if it were of no importance, which was another pointer to just how Westernized she had become. 'Getting back to Chris—when he does fall in love with you, and you get to work on him, be careful.' Lefki wagged a finger at her friend, her mouth curved with amusement. 'It's knowing when to stop that's the important thing. Chris will be like Paul,' she continued knowledgeably, 'He'll tolerate so much and no more, so take heed of what I've said and be careful!'

After the wedding reception Chris and Judy flew to Athens, where they stayed the night. The hotel was in Constitution Square and Chris had previously booked a magnificent suite of rooms.

They entered the lift, accompanied by a porter carrying most of their luggage, and only then did Judy seem to become really alive to the position she was in. This stranger was her husband, with rights over her; she must submit to the demands he would make on her, must respect him and obey him. She looked up; his eyes flickered and she knew he read her thoughts. Judy blushed and a smile of sardonic amusement touched his lips.

She tried to calculate how many hours she had spent in his company; not more than the twenty-four that make up a day and a night. She thought of Ronnie, whom she loved and from whom she had even been denied the bitter-sweet agony of a final goodbye. Judy felt she hated this man who had offered for her; she felt she hated her grandfather too. Tears sprang to her eyes as she dwelt on what she had been denied by the premature death of her parents. Her own life ... what was it worth?

They were suddenly in the bedroom; their suitcases had been put down and they were alone. Judy moved to the window and looked out. There were the familiar street traders—the little cart where one could buy *koulouria*, the rings of bread with those delicious seeds

37

on top; the sponge-seller and the inevitable bootblack. The Greeks were always having their shoes cleaned—perhaps it was because there was so much dust about——

'What are you thinking?' Her husband's voice, close to her ear. Judy stiffened and would have moved away, but her shoulders were suddenly grasped and she was turned around so that she faced her husband. 'Those beautiful eyes are so dreamy and far away,' he said, looking deeply into them. She stood quite still, afraid to reveal her aversion in case she aroused his anger. How dark he was! And how inaccessible. If only she could talk to him and plead with him and be sure he would listen, and soften and understand.

'I wasn't thinking of anything in particular,' she faltered. 'The—the street-traders always—always fascinate me.'

He looked down into the square.

'You've been here often?'

'Only twice.' He was still holding her; his hands were warm and she didn't like them touching her. 'I have a friend who lives in Athens.'

'You might like to visit her some time.'

'I visited her several weeks ago...' She tailed off because his eyes were glinting like steel.

'Of course. Your frandfather told me you met this Englishman on the plane when you were returning to Cyprus.'

She nodded.

'Yes, I did.'

'And fell in love with him.' A statement, spoken in harsh and strangely bitter tones. 'It's a great pity you were allowed this freedom. Your life would be happier had you not met him.'

She put a hand to her throat, nodding again.

'I suppose it would.'

Suddenly he bent and kissed her on the lips. She closed her eyes and thought of Ronnie—and then burst into tears. Was it nerves? she vaguely wondered. She knew she was tensed and overwrought, afraid of the night and of the slow, agonizing hours before it came. Chris brought out a handkerchief and to her astonishment his voice held no hint of impatience as he said,

'Now what can these tears be for? Ronnie, I presume.' He sighed on answering his own question. 'Yes, it's a great pity you were allowed that freedom.' He dried her eyes, and she looked up at him wonderingly. He was no different—still cold and unapproachable, and yet there was an element of gentleness in the way he dried her eyes, and in the way he gazed down at her. Would he listen now—if she told him of her fears? She spoke his name falteringly,

'Chris . . .'

'Yes, Judy?'

She swallowed hard and then,

'I don't want—I don't want . . .' She felt the tears behind her eyes again and blinked rapidly to hold them back. Chris's patience would not stretch too far, she thought.

'Yes, Judy,' he said in tones suddenly crisp. 'What is it you don't want?'

'We're strangers,' she whispered, and all her fear was in her voice, mingling with her plea for understanding. 'If you would—would give me a little time to get to know you?'

Silence. Down below the lights were appearing as the brief twilight followed the rapid sinking of the sun. Chris moved away; she sensed the sudden tautness of him and wondered if this meant that she could hope.

'Why,' he asked in tight emphatic tones, 'do you think I married you?'

Judy sagged.

'So you won't wait a little while?'

'A bridegroom doesn't usually wait a little while.'

'No—but our marriage is different. I'm English.'

That appeared to amuse him. She was glad his manner had changed because that tautness only added to her fears, although she could not have said why.

'You're not English,' he corrected. 'Your mother was a Greek Cypriot. However, that's of no matter. What has nationality to do with it anyway?'

'English girls fall in love. What I mean is, they know their husbands well before the marriage——'

'So I believe,' he cut in drily, and the colour flooded her face.

'I really mean,' Judy persevered after a while, 'that, to me, it doesn't seem right to—to——' She broke off, colouring up again, and he finished for her,

'To marry a stranger?'

She nodded.

'The marrying part is all right,' she said innocently. 'But it's the——' She glanced at the bed and quite unexpectedly he laughed. She was fascinated by the change in his face. Yes, she had been right when she asserted that he was more handsome than Paul.

'So it's the making love that troubles you, is it?'

She turned away, but for some strange reason her embarrassment was not as great as she would have expected it to be.

'You knew it was, right from the start, didn't you? And you've been enjoying my discomfiture.'

'You know, Judy,' he said, coming to her again and bringing her round to face him, 'it's going to be delightful being married to you. I'm sure we shall get along famously together.' His lips met hers and again she stood there, meek, unmoving, thinking of Ronnie. 'No response?' Amusement touched the hard outline of his mouth. 'What is it, my little Judy—shyness, or merely that you dislike having me near you?'

So he sensed her aversion. Perhaps he was remembering that she loved someone else. Judy wished she had the courage to mention this, for then perhaps he would not kiss her—or even...

She could not bear to think of the night and she switched her thoughts to Lefki instead, and to the way she had managed Paul. 'It's the way you start,' Lefki had said. 'If you begin by being timid and allowing yourself to be downtrodden then you're lost immediately.' No being mastered for Lefki. If she did not want to do what her husband asked she just disobeyed him, and although his reaction led to quarrels Lefki held firm and in the end Paul capitulated.

Judy looked up at Chris; he had asked her a question, but she made no attempt to answer it. She was so deeply engrossed in a recollection of that conversation with Lefki. One had to know how far to go, it appeared, and a pucker of bewilderment creased her brow. How did one estimate the distance one could go with safety? It worked better, too, if one's husband were in love—and of course Chris was not in love. He had seen Judy and, desiring her, had proceeded in the orthodox way and offered for her. Yes, it worked better if one's husband were in love, Lefki had admitted that. Nevertheless, it could still work if one's husband's only interest was desire, as was the case with Chris.

It was how you started.... If you did not want something you must openly disobey your husband.... Over and over again Lefki's words repeated themselves as Judy stood there, fear and courage battling for supremacy. To fight as Lefki had done took a great deal of initial courage, which Judy had not possessed at the time she was being forced into marriage, but now... If Lefki could do it, then why couldn't she? If you did

41

not want to do something . . . Judy did not want Chris to stay with her tonight—not in fact until she knew him better. Her eyes still gazed into his. What could he do to her if she defied him? He could not murder her; nor could he beat her, as Kyria's husband beat her. No, not in the hotel, he couldn't, because she would scream and someone would come.

'I'm not letting you stay with me tonight,' she said—and blinked. Had she really uttered those words? It would seem like it, judging by her husband's expression.

'What did you say?' he asked unbelievingly.

Judy went white. But her determination was now strong. She was married to Chris and the marriage was permanent. Ronnie was not for her and she was resigned to the fact that she must try to forget him. Fate had sent her to Cyprus when she was young; by the customs of the island she had been forced to accept the husband her grandfather had chosen for her. But she was British, and in any case, even if she were a Cypriot she would still have learned from Lefki, who, herself a Cypriot, had found the courage to lift herself from the level of vassalage to that of her husband's equal. Judy decided she could do likewise; she also decided she must begin at once, and although her heart pulsated quite abnormally she managed to articulate her words with a clarity that amazed her.

'I said I'm not letting you stay with me tonight,' she repeated, but then she added, 'Later, when I know you better, I might change my mind.'

The silence of amazement filled the room. She had stunned him! Judy felt quite proud of herself in spite of her husband's dark incredulous face above her and the glowering expression in his eyes.

'You—might—change—your—mind?' Each word was pronounced with astounded precision. 'How very obliging of you. What am I supposed to do now? Express my humble thanks and bow myself out—backwards?'

Judy blinked uncertainly, rather at a loss. What would normally be the next move? How would Lefki deal with this situation? But Lefki had wanted Paul, so in her case a situation such as this would never have arisen. Judy's heartbeats were still racing, and no wonder, so darkly threatening was her husband's countenance. But she must not weaken. It was her fate to stay married to Chris and she intended to be his partner, not his possession. True, Chris did appear rather frightening, but hadn't Lefki firmly asserted that all men were basically the same? Lie down, she had said, and they would trample all over you; stand up to them and they'd usually see eye to eye simply because it was less wearing than being for ever in a tussle with you.

'It's only because I don't know you,' she began to explain. 'I don't think it ought to be yet. If we remain just friends, and—well, keep company, like they do in Western countries, and like I would have done had I been brought up in England, then we shall gradually get to know one another and everything will be—er—normal,' she ended vaguely.

He had moved away, but his eyes never left her face. She stood with her back to the window, a slender figure of nymph-like charm and captivating allure. In her innocence and determination to fight for emancipation she didn't stop to think what she was asking. And perhaps had she known just how tempting she appeared to this dark Greek she would not have been so sublimely confident of herself. Strangely, though, his features began to relax and Judy felt sure she detected a hint of amusement enter those dark metallic eyes. Perception was there too, and she had the odd conviction that he had guessed, quite suddenly, what she was about. What she did not know was that her own eyes still contained the shade of fear . . . and that her husband had noticed this and realized she was very young and innocent.

'Tidy yourself up,' he said. 'We'll go somewhere and eat.'

She blinked at him. No argument or attempt at domination? How easy it all was! Why hadn't she asserted herself before? She could so easily have broken the engagement, she now decided. Had she stood firm Chris would have given her her way—and she would have been free to marry Ronnie. Somehow, though, it all seemed too good to be true and she was forced to say,

'But we haven't settled this matter.' She hoped she sounded businesslike and brisk and she searched his face to discover how he was taking this. All she saw was a kindling of his eyes as he said abruptly,

'We're going out!' And, remembering there was a point beyond which it was imprudent to go, Judy returned with sudden meekness,

'Yes, Chris, I'll get changed.'

This she did in the bathroom, putting on a tailored dress in white linen, and white sandals. A white Alice band round her hair made her look about fifteen, and Chris, emerging from the other bathroom, stood by the door for a moment, looking at her and shaking his head.

'Perhaps,' he said, giving a little sigh, 'I should have waited even longer.'

At this surprising comment her eyes opened very wide. But before she could think of anything to say in return he had picked up her coat from the bed and was holding it out for her to put on.

This little attention was unusual, and it set her wondering if perhaps she had made one big mistake in thinking he meant to subjugate her and treat her as a possession. But all Greek men treated their wives as possessions, as did Cypriots. No, she had not made a mistake. He was no different from the rest and she must never weaken in her efforts at 'man-management' as Lefki had described it.

They went out into the lighted square, and sauntered through the streets until Chris found the *taverna* he wanted. The meal was excellent, and after it was over they remained in the garden drinking wine and watching the Greek dancers leaping and twisting to the accompaniment of a *bouzouki* and a guitar. The gardens were a romantic setting, with coloured lights twinkling from the trees and a crescent moon poised in a purple sky from which a myriad stars looked down. Warm balmy air and a soft perfumed breeze; colour and music and the sort of gaiety and abandon found only in Greece.

To Judy's surprise she was reasonably happy—until her husband said it was time they were returning to the hotel.

'We have to be up early tomorrow in order to catch the ferry,' he added. They were going to his home on the island of Hydra, one of the 'Siren isles' of the Saronic Gulf. There they would live, on this small, almost barren island, one-time home of bold, buccaneering men but now the haunt of Greek millionaire ship-owners, and painters and writers. Practically the whole of the population lived close to the picturesque little harbour; only the mansions of the rich occupied magnificent sites on the hillsides to the west of the port.

In complete silence Judy and her husband walked back to the hotel. Had she really achieved anything? she wondered, looking up at him the moment they entered their sitting-room. His dark face was expressionless, and yet she sensed a sort of animal desire which he was striving to suppress. Massive, he seemed against her, and powerful. How could she even contemplate engaging such a man in combat, let alone expect the spoils of victory to be hers? He could pick her up like a small toy, and her struggles would not only be futile but laughable. She was afraid, terribly afraid; her fear was seen by him again and, turning abruptly, he left her, only to return a few minutes later carrying a pillow and a blanket. She stared, speechless, as he placed the pillow on the couch and then spread out the blanket.

'Wh-what are you d-doing?' she stammered, quite unable to believe her eyes.

He straightened up, his mouth compressed and yet in his eyes the sort of expression that portrayed resigned amusement.

'Isn't this what you wanted?' and without waiting for an answer, 'I'd have booked another bedroom had I known. However, this will suffice for one night.' Taking her face in his hands, he bent his head and kissed her on the mouth. 'Good night, Judy, pleasant dreams.' She did not move and he gave her a little tap. 'Off you go before I change my mind,' he recommended, and she prudently did as she was told.

How perfectly simple it all had been, she thought as she slid down between the cool white sheets a short while later. So fortunate that she had questioned Lefki and learned about 'man-management'. Just to think, she had told him she was not letting him stay tonight and he had meekly taken himself into the sitting-room where he would sleep on the couch. It really was quite incredible, because his personality had always seemed so overpowering. Judy yawned and turned her face into the pillow. Lefki was so right when she said all men were basically the same. . . .

46

CHAPTER THREE

THE island of Hydra rose like some lovely jewel from a sea of dazzling blue. Above the spectacular harbour with its brightly coloured caïques and blue and white houses and shops rose the barren rocky mass of Mount Prophet Ilias, while gleaming in the sun were the impressive white mansions of the rich, rising one above another and standing on precipitous cliffs above the more humble houses of the village, which were arranged like an amphitheatre around the circular little harbour.

'It's beautiful!' exclaimed Judy impulsively, turning to look up at her husband, standing beside her at the rail of the ship. He merely allowed her a flicker of attention before returning his gaze to the island, which was coming so close now that the whitewashed cobbled streets could clearly be seen. Judy flushed, because of her husband's disinterest in her. She thought of the silent breakfast, the cool, impersonal remarks he had passed when they were in the taxi travelling to the Piræus to catch the ferry, and then silence again during the voyage to his island home. 'Can you see your house from here?' she asked perseveringly.

He turned a mild stare in her direction, and nodded.

'It's the highest one on the west of the harbour.' A negligent gesture of his hand indicated the gleaming white mansion whose marble fountains could be seen sparkling in the sunlight. 'It's called Salaris House.'

'That one?' She was used to luxury, her grandfather's house being one of the most outstanding in Kyrenia, but on seeing the imposing edifice reclining on the mountainside she opened her eyes wide. 'It looks wonderful!' she breathed, rather awed.

Her husband said nothing, but his detached stare remained upon her. She frowned inwardly. For some quite incomprehensible reason she was troubled by an uncomfortable little pang of guilt—nothing serious, but it was the sort of feeling she had experienced as a child when some misdemeanour had been committed and her grandfather was vexed with her.

They were very close now to the little old-world port and Judy picked out one or two grey-stone houses, tall and architecturally very different from the cluster of little cubic houses which seemed from this angle to be touching one another.

'Why are those houses so different—the grey ones, I mean?' she asked, still wanting him to hold a conversation with her, although she could not have said why.

'They were the homes of piratical traders who went in for lavish entertaining two hundred or so years ago. As a matter of fact mine is one, but it's had many alterations and additions over the years, some of which I've had done myself.'

'Were they Greek, these traders?'

'No, Albanians.' His eyes still lingered on her, their expression inscrutable. What was he thinking? It was impossible to guess, but she did wonder, a little fearfully, if he were regretting his calm acceptance of her decision last night. That he *had* accepted was a circumstance which to her surprise had kept her awake for hours pondering over it. He had married her for desire, that went without saying, and from the very first Judy had accepted that. So why, after having offered for her and married her for the sole purpose of possessing her, had he, on their very first night, meekly accepted her word as law? It just did not make sense, even though Judy had been firm and determined because, as Lefki

48

had said, she must start right if she were to attain the status of her husband's equal. Chris was so confident and self-possessed, so obviously masterful even though as yet he had made no real attempt at mastery. On learning of her little affair with Ronnie he had fairly made her tremble in her shoes and it seemed so very odd that, simply because she herself had gained a little confidence and courage, Chris should instantly lose his. No, it certainly did not make sense, despite Lefki's assertion that men were all alike and would give in rather than become engaged in a tussle with their wives.

'Here we are.' Chris's voice broke into her reverie and she turned to him. 'Are you ready for a long climb?'

'We have to walk?'

'Naturally.'

'You haven't a car?'

'Not here. A car wouldn't be any use to get up there—even were there a road.'

Judy soon learned that the 'roads' were lanes so steep that they were stepped, and she seemed to have covered hundreds of these steps before she came at last to the great white house on the plateau cut into the side of the hill. It had thirty-eight rooms, Chris told her when on entering the massive hall she stared in bewilderment first at all the doors on the ground floor and then at the grand staircase leading to the upper apartments.

'Thirty-eight!' She stared at him, feeling smaller than ever. The hint of a smile curved his lips. He said with cool impersonality,

'My sister and her husband have a suite of rooms here, and so does my mother. They come during the summer for a long stay.'

His sister and mother.... Floria was nineteen and had been married a year. Judy had seen her only once, when she came to Cyprus with Chris for a holiday. Judy had not been able to attend her wedding, as she was at school at that time, in France. Chris's mother she had never met, nor his father. They were separated, a rare occurrence with Greeks. Judy had never learned the reason for the separation, for Chris had never offered one, and Judy, looking upon him as a stranger, had naturally refrained from broaching the subject.

Judy turned her head as two Greek youths entered the hall. They were bringing in the luggage, having picked it up at the quay.

'Down there.' Chris spoke abruptly and put his hand in his pocket. He paid them and they went out, thanking him with a smile that revealed a flash of white teeth. Chris clapped his hands imperiously and a man-servant appeared. 'My wife, Spiros,' he said briefly.

The man smiled and said,

'Welcome, Madam Voulis. *Isasthe poli haritomeni!*'

She blushed, unconsciously glancing up at her husband. His gaze was cool, sardonic, and her blush deepened.

'*Efharistó poli,*' she murmured even as Chris was telling Spiros to take their suitcases up to their rooms.

'So Spiros thinks you're pretty,' commented Chris in a rather bored voice when a few minutes later they were in Judy's room, having followed Spiros upstairs. 'I must admit your blush was quite charming, and you thanked him with the sort of smile you have never shown to me.'

They were standing in the middle of the room; vaguely, Judy was aware of a magnificent view of the town and the harbour and the great expanse of blue unmoving sea. Chris was regarding her critically now, as if Spiros's declaration that she was very pretty had given him something to think about. For her part, Judy just stared up at him, her lovely blue eyes very wide and innocent, her lips parted, and, although she did not know it, almost irresistibly inviting to this stranger husband of hers.

What was this odd note in his voice as he spoke of the smile she had given to Spiros? Was it pique? Undoubtedly ... and yet why should Chris be piqued? It certainly wasn't her smiles he wanted....

'Are your relatives here at present?' she inquired conversationally.

'Floria will be here in about a week's time and her husband will follow shortly afterwards. He has business to attend to in Athens and can't come just whenever he wants to. Mother will arrive in a couple of weeks or so. We all gather here for two or three months in the summer.'

'So we're on our own for a week?' The words broke automatically and his lips twisted with a hint of mockery.

'Quite alone, but for the servants.' Judy eyed him uncertainly. He seemed faintly amused, yet at the same time exasperated to a small degree. However, his voice was cool and unemotional as he added, 'Have no fear, Judy, you won't need to call upon them for help.'

Her face grew hotter even while elation swept over her. She fell to wondering why the girls of the East were so downtrodden when this man-management was so ridiculously easy. Of course, as Lefki said, it was the way one started. Because they had been indoctrinated for generations with the idea of male superiority the women of the East automatically offered no resistance. How foolish they were! Someone should give them lessons, she thought, just as Lefki had given Judy a lesson.

Chris turned away and her eyes followed him. The door between the two rooms was slightly ajar and he pushed it open and disappeared into his own room.

51

The door closed; Judy smiled to herself. She must write to Lefki and thank her.

As the days passed a small element of friendship developed between Judy and Chris, but otherwise theirs was an unimpassioned union of prosaic domesticity. During the mornings Chris would withdraw to his study, a vast and luxuriously furnished apartment with a terrace from where could be seen the colourful little harbour with its immaculate houses and shops and its congestion of little caïques and pleasure craft of all kinds. Judy would be consulted by the cook, Julia, a dark and stolid Greek woman who had been in the employ of Chris's father for many years, coming to Chris on the break-up of his father's marriage five years previously.

'What is the menu for lunch?' Julia would ask, a notebook held between her fingers and a businesslike expression on her face.

'Lunch?' Judy faltered on the first occasion. At home in Cyprus she had never been consulted about such things. 'Er—what do you suggest?'

The woman shrugged.

'It's for you to plan the menu, madam.'

'Yes. . . .' And Judy had then told Julia to leave it for a while so that she could give the matter some thought. But immediately on the cook's departure Judy had gone in to her husband.

'What would you like for lunch?' she inquired, glancing at the array of papers on his desk. One was a picture of a magnificent white pleasure cruiser and she wondered if it belonged to him.

Chris threw her a frowning glance.

'Meals, my dear, are entirely your department.' And he added crisply, 'I do draw the line somewhere.'

Draw the line? What a peculiar thing to say! A tiny

frown of perplexity settled on Judy's wide brow. There was no doubt about it, her husband did act in the strangest way, and say the strangest things. It occurred to Judy all at once that although she was succeeding in her fight for equality with her husband she was having much less success with her desire to understand his temperament.

During the afternoons she and Chris would swim in the flower-bordered pool in the garden, or sit on the lawn or terrace enjoying the sun. When doing this latter they would read, and sometimes, feeling her husband's concentrated gaze fixed upon her, Judy would raise her head to see him regarding her with an expression half frowning, half amused. What went on in that mind of his? With the passing of each day Judy found her curiosity increasing.

'We'll go for a walk,' he said one day after lunch. 'You haven't seen much of the island yet.'

Somehow, the idea of a walk with him was pleasant and it was with unusual eagerness that she sped upstairs and changed into a very short cotton skirt and a sleeveless, low-necked sun-top. Her hair was a glorious mass of gold falling in soft and tender abandon on to her shoulders, which were bare except for the narrowest of straps. She had bought this little outfit in Paris; there were shorts to match, but these she had not put on.

Lightly she ran down the stairs, hair flying, nymph-like and very lovely. Chris was standing in the hall waiting for her, his head bent as if he were endeavouring to unravel the pattern of the mosaic of black and white veined marbles with which the floor was elaborately paved. At the sound of her feet he looked up; something moved in his throat, but his glance appeared to be entirely lacking in interest. Therefore it came as a surprise when he said,

'Very charming. I believe I have the most beautiful wife in the whole of Greece.' Adorably she blushed, thinking that life with Chris might be pleasant in the extreme once she had established herself as his partner in the way Lefki had done with Paul. 'What have you got on underneath that skirt?' he calmly inquired, and Judy gave a start.

'Underneath...?' Unconsciously she touched a fold of the skirt, her cheeks hotter than ever. 'Nothing—— Oh, I mean——!' Mercifully he cut her short, his dark eyes kindling with amusement.

'Unless I'm mistaken, you have a very attractive pair of shorts to go with that top?' She just stared, endeavouring to regain her composure, and he added, 'No, you haven't worn them here, but you did when you were in France; your grandfather showed me some snapshots you sent him.'

'Oh...' she quivered as he paused for a space. 'Did he?' Judy had not known that her fiancé had seen the snapshots, but obviously he had. She would have expected him to be annoyed, or uninterested. But he was neither.

'Go and put them on,' he ordered quietly. 'I'll wait on the terrace for you.'

She looked doubtfully at him. Eastern he was, with the chiselled granite-like severity portrayed in the face of the average Greek aristocrat, but he appeared to have thrown aside the old-fashioned idea that a woman's body should be demurely covered. Every single day he gave her a surprise, she thought.

'Wear them, to go walking with you?' she queried, still a shade uncertain.

He nodded.

'And leave the skirt off.'

'Oh, but—when I wear the shorts for walking I just open the skirt——' She indicated the front. 'There are

54

buttons, you see.'

'Yes, I see.' He stifled a yawn. 'Leave it off,' he said again, and went out on to the terrace.

Judy ran back upstairs and it was not until she had emerged from the house on to the terrace, and noted the look of satisfaction on her husband's face, that she asked herself whether or not she should have obeyed him. Submission to his will must be avoided at all costs—but the trouble was that Judy had no idea at all about that point beyond which she must not go.

'That's better.' Chris's eyes roved over her, in the sort of appraising manner with which all Greek men examined women. Judy was used to it; she read his thoughts with accuracy—and somehow felt a tinge of desolation. Other men could look at her like that, but she wished her husband wouldn't. But how did she want him to look at her? A frown of bewilderment touched her brow because she could find no answer to her question. 'Why the dark look?' he suddenly asked, and her face cleared.

'I was thinking, but it's nothing important.'

'It must have been important to make you frown like that. Tell me.'

Judy did not want to reply, but Chris's mouth was set and his gaze demanding. She told the truth, saying that it was the way he looked at her.

'The way I look at you?' he repeated blankly. 'What exactly do you mean by that?'

She swallowed, wondering how to answer him without herself suffering embarrassment. Besides, she had a shrewd suspicion that he knew what she meant and that his puzzlement was feigned.

'It doesn't matter,' she said at last hastily.

He hesitated a moment in indecision and then, with an air of indifference,

'Come, we shall walk over to the other side of the

harbour and see a friend of mine.'

They went down, first, towards the harbour, traversing cobblestoned alleys the majority of which were stepped. The cobblestones were whitewashed almost every day, the houses were also white, with the traditional blue shutters found on practically every Greek house. The harbour was neat and clean and many graceful sailing craft stood moored, gently swayed by the prevailing north-west wind which could at times be troublesome to sailors, many of whom, when handling pleasure craft, preferred the safer port of Spetsai, an island some short distance away to the south-west. The whiteness and cleanness, combined with the masses of flowers—roses and jasmine, hibiscus and oleanders—gave the scene a gay and colourful aspect in spite of the immaculate air that seemed to typify this particular Greek island.

Judy trotted beside her husband in the sunshine, feeling far less unhappy than she had anticipated on her wedding day when, standing there beside Chris, before the smiling bearded priest, she had made her vows in faltering reluctant tones, her heart a leaden weight within her. At that time she had looked with overpowering dread to the time, only hours away, when her formidable bridegroom would demand and take from her what he had patiently waited over two years to attain. But, strengthened by her new-found courage and determination not to enter into that state of slavery to which all her friends but Lefki had resigned themselves, Judy had won the first vital round without receiving as much as a scratch. It was not that she meant to continue in this way; she intended 'keeping company' with her husband until some sort of affection entered into their relationship—love being quite out of the question because Ronnie had her heart, even though she sternly told herself she must

56

forget him—and then, if in addition to the affection existing between them, Chris had also accepted her as his equal, she would, as she had half promised on her wedding night, 'change her mind'.

On reaching the shops in the harbour Chris bought her a box of chocolates. It was the first present he had bought her—she did not count the diamond bracelet he had given her for a wedding present because she had not liked it at all and it was now in its case in one of the drawers in her room—and she raised her lovely eyes as she thanked him in husky tones. He slipped the chocolates in her bag and they walked on, towards the white *taverna* with its blue shutters and tables set out on the pavement. Men idled on the chairs, drinking the inevitable Turkish coffee from minute cups which they filled up now and then from the glasses of water which in Greece always accompany the coffee. Fishermen had spread their nets to dry in the sun, and were sitting in little groups, gossiping and clicking their worry beads, but they all looked up with interest at seeing Chris with his new wife. Greetings were exchanged between them and Chris, and then the usual examination of Judy, from her sandal-clad feet to the top of her head. She was used to this and she did not blush; Chris turned his head to note her reaction and a hint of amusement touched his lips at her immunity to the stares of the men. He was not in the least jealous, she thought, remembering how angry Ronnie would become when the Cypriots allowed their eyes to rove over her in this way.

A little farther along the quay several youths were standing around two men who were pounding an octopus. She shuddered and again her husband appeared to be amused.

'You eat octopus, surely?' he asked.

She shook her head.

57

'I've never even tasted it.'

'They're delicious. You have the tentacles fried in butter.'

Judy said nothing. She was used to Greek food, naturally, because it was eaten all the time in Cyprus, but she had never been able to eat octopus. There was something revolting about those tentacles, and besides, she did not care for the way the octopus were tenderized—by banging them repeatedly on the rocks or stones, and then rubbing them until a great lather appeared.

A cruise ship was in and masses of tourists surged on to the quay; shopkeepers stood outside their doors, ready to do business, selling their souvenirs and postcards and of course the lovely sponges which the sponge-divers of the island brought from the rich fishing grounds of North Africa.

Judy and Chris left the port at last and began climbing one little flight of cobbled steps after another until they reached the house of Chris's friend.

'You walked?' he said after Chris had introduced him to Judy. 'I always use a donkey myself.' His house was not nearly so magnificent as that of Chris; nevertheless, it was on the scale of a mansion, with an immense drawing-room to which he led them after they had spent a few minutes chatting on the terrace. 'So this is Judy.' He looked her over once more, and appeared to like what he saw. 'Chris waited a long while for you. You should be flattered.' George Cozakis brought forward a chair for her and she sat down, her eyes remaining appreciatively on him. He was slight of build with laughing eyes and a ready smile. His hair was brown—not nearly so dark as that of Chris. His age, Judy estimated, was about the same as that of her husband—twenty-eight or nine. He was handsome in a softer, more gentle way than Chris, although there was

58

a firmness to his features, nevertheless. He smiled often, unlike Chris, whose face was unmoving, reflecting the reserve which was an inherent part of him. George also talked a good deal, while Chris remained quiet, listening. George openly flattered Judy and Chris did not seem to mind; George informed her that she was the last in a long line of beautiful girls who had aspired to become the wife of the wealthy Chrisalis, but this time Chris did seem to mind.

'Don't exaggerate, George,' he interrupted with a frown. 'You'll have Judy thinking I'm a profligate.'

She looked at him and for the first time wondered about his past life. He would have girls, she felt sure, and as he also had a home in Athens that would not be difficult, for there life was freer than in the villages and islands of Greece; girls went about alone and could, therefore, find men-friends. A long line.... How many? She frowned then and recalled his fury on learning about Ronnie. How unfair it all was, she mused, her frown deepening. A man could do what he liked—have dozens of women before marriage—but a girl must keep herself for her husband, because if he discovered after marriage that she was not chaste he could divorce her immediately and she would never live down the disgrace and shame, which would not only affect the girl herself, but her family as well.

Chris's eyes were riveted on her; he was plainly endeavouring to read her thoughts. A small flush rose to highlight the lovely contours of her face and she saw a movement at the side of his neck. His gaze, however, took on a hint of mocking amusement and she guessed at once that her blush was responsible for his sudden humour.

'Exaggerate?' George's eyebrows rose a fraction. 'There was Stella and Maroula and Elli. Then you had the two English ones and the Swede—I'll bet she

59

taught you a thing or two,' he laughed. 'Then the next thing I knew you were almost married to Corinne Moore—she's here, by the way——'

'My dear George,' interrupted Chris with a yawn, 'I'm quite sure Judy doesn't want to sit here listening to all this rubbish which flows so glibly from your tongue.' He looked at his wife. 'Take no heed, my dear. George just loves to hear himself talk.'

Judy remained silent. That George spoke the truth she did not for a moment doubt. She considered it in very bad taste for him to reel off the names of her husband's previous girl-friends, and yet she could not dislike George. On the contrary, it was Chris on whom her disgusted gaze came at last to rest. His brows rose then, arrogantly ... and could it be warningly? This idea brought a lift to Judy's chin. He must not adopt that manner with her, this gesture was meant to indicate, and Chris's eyes glinted darkly. At that Judy swallowed, realizing it was going to be most difficult to maintain her new-found courage—but maintain it she must if she were ever to attain the status she desired, the status which would automatically have been hers had she been brought up in England, and married one of her own people.

George was clapping his hands for the servant and this relieved the tension that was building up between Judy and Chris. George asked what they wanted to drink and the order was given on the appearance of the manservant.

The refreshments brought, the two men fell into a business conversation as they drank and Judy began to dwell on what George had said about Chris's having been almost married to someone called Corinne Moore. English, apparently ... and was he really almost married to her? If so, what had happened? She was here now, George had been saying when Chris had interrupted him.

'I think I'll go to Venice to see the *Andromeda* set sail on her first trip,' George was saying, and Judy's thoughts were diverted from this unknown Corinne Moore to the conversation going on between the two men. 'It's all very ordinary to you, Chris, but this is the first ship built since I joined the firm. I'd like to take the cruise, even, but I'm far too busy.'

'You can take a cruise on her another time,' remarked Chris without much interest.

'But this is her maiden voyage, and that's why I'm so eager to take the trip.' But he shrugged then, and repeated that he was far too busy.

Later, on their way home, Judy said hesitantly,

'I gathered you have a new ship being built?'

'She's already built; takes her first voyage a month from now.'

'How many ships have you got?' she inquired curiously.

'I, personally, don't have any. It's a company.'

'But you're a ship-owner—Grandfather said you were.' It struck her as all wrong that her entire information about her husband had come from her grandfather. Chris should have talked to her, and told her about himself—about his childhood and his family and his business. But of course women from the East were treated as slaves, and one did not confide in a slave. Well, she was not from the East—and she would continue with the good work of bringing this home to her husband.

'I suppose I do own some ships,' he conceded. 'But, as I've said, it's a firm, so everything is shared, as it were.' He sounded bored, as if the explanation was a little wearing, because she was only a woman. Once more her pretty little chin lifted. She recalled that Lefki loved travel and that she also had no difficulty in getting her husband to take her travelling.

'I think I would like to sail on the *Andromeda*,' she said and, as on another occasion, she blinked, amazed at her own daring.

They were climbing the last few steps before reaching the start of the terraced garden surrounding the house and in his surprise Chris almost stopped.

'Your place,' he said at last cuttingly, 'is with your husband, not gadding about all over the Mediterranean!'

'Oh, I didn't mean to go on my own——'

'You didn't? I'm relieved to hear it!'

'I thought we might go together,' she persisted, passing in front of him as they reached the gate. 'Where is the *Andromeda* going?'

'Her destination need not trouble you. You won't be on board.' He turned to close the gate because old Andonis would leave his donkey untethered and it wandered into the garden and ate the flowers.

'Lefki's husband takes her travelling all over the place.' Judy twisted round to gaze up at him with a sort of winsome expression in her beautiful blue eyes. 'I would very much like to travel, too.'

'Lefki? Who's she?'

'My great friend. She was at our wedding, but perhaps you didn't notice because there was such a crush. She married a rich man and he takes her everywhere she wants to go.'

'He does?'. They were in the courtyard and Chris stopped. They were in a setting of marble fountains and ornate wrought iron, of exotic flowers whose perfume was scattered over the whole hillside by the soft warm breeze blowing in from the sea far down below. 'Tell me more about this Lefki,' he invited. 'Is her husband a Cypriot?'

'Yes; Paul. But he doesn't boss her about as they

usually do,' Judy informed him with adorable naïveté. 'He treats Lefki as an equal—just as if they were a couple from England or France. And whenever she wants to travel he takes her. Do you know,' she went on confidingly, yet with a touch of awe, 'Lefki spent three thousand pounds on Georgian silver the last time Paul took her to London!'

To her surprise Chris was not particularly impressed by her words. Nevertheless, he did say in dry and pointed tones,

'Well, don't you get any ideas of spending three thousand pounds on Georgian silver—or any ideas about going to London, even,' he added inflexibly.

She bit her lip. Her husband noted the action and an odd expression entered his eyes, an expression which brought back a fleeting vision of his face when, on their wedding night, she had looked at him in the hotel bedroom and felt instinctively that he knew what she was about.

'I don't particularly want to buy Georgian silver,' she told him accommodatingly, unaware that the conversation was entering into a humorous phase. 'You see, I don't know much about it, so I might be cheated.'

Chris regarded her inscrutably for a space and then, glancing round, he moved towards the wicker chairs which had been placed in the shade of the lemon trees growing on the fringe of garden adjoining the courtyard. He sat down, leaning back rather in the slouching manner of Greek men when they were idling their time away in the *tavernas* or by the waterfront. A very deep frown creased his brow and to her surprise his lips twitched. He straightened up and said,

'Again you need not worry. You won't be cheated because there's no possibility of my giving you three thousand pounds to run around London with.'

His sarcasm offended her and she set her mouth. At

this defiant little gesture his eyes opened very wide, and his dark head tilted in a way that spelled mastery and warning. Judy moistened her lips. Mastery was the one vital thing she meant to fight, but what move must she now make in order to avoid taking a downward step?

'I've just said I don't want to buy silver,' she returned at last, moving closer to him and looking straight at him. 'But I *do* want to travel.'

A small silence then and she sat down, waiting rather breathlessly for his reaction to her words. But he said nothing and she presently added, more to end the oppressive silence than anything else, 'If Lefki can travel, then I don't see why I can't as well.'

He emerged from his thoughtful silence and again she saw the humorous twitching of his lips.

'Lefki....' He repeated the name musingly. 'You should have introduced me to her at the wedding. I'm sure she must be a most unusual and interesting young woman.'

Judy glanced uncertainly at him. Was he teasing her? But no. Chris was always grave and detached. Today he was also a little disconcerting, and for the first time she wished he were like Ronnie—transparent and accommodating. They would get along fine then, she felt sure, and perhaps she would relent and allow him to be a proper husband to her.

'She is unusual,' agreed Judy at last as Chris sat there in an attitude of waiting. 'Unusual for a Cypriot girl, that is. You see, she has achieved this equal status with her husband.'

'So I gather,' was the dry comment from Chris. 'She's your great friend, you said?'

Judy nodded. Her gaze was concentrated on the glorious view across the terraced grounds of the house to the slopes below and the town and harbour lower

64

down still. From the trees close by the sound of cicadas filled the air, which was fast becoming hot and sultry, for June was almost at an end.

'Lefki went to school in France, just as I did,' supplied Judy. 'So we have much in common.'

Chris lifted his eyes, allowed them to settle on his wife's face for a moment and then, in the same dry tones,

'So it would appear.'

The brief remark seemed to hold a wealth of hidden meaning and Judy blinked at him in an inquiring, puzzled sort of way. But he merely sat back in his chair, regarding her through narrowed eyes, and she suddenly felt at a loss for words. Certainly he was disconcerting today, and he seemed to be playing some sort of game with her, a game from which he derived a certain amount of pleasure not untinged with amusement. The silence threatened to become uncomfortable and she said with rather exaggerated carelessness,

'You've switched the conversation, Chris. I was talking about travel. I asked you where the *Andromeda* was going.'

He was not listening. His eyes were on a pink-clad figure climbing the steps up the hillside. Following the direction of his gaze, Judy took in the tall slim figure of a girl of about twenty-five years of age. Dark-haired and tanned to a deep golden brown, she was obviously not a holidaymaker from the gleaming white cruise ship resting at anchor in the calm blue waters of the gulf below, for she knew her way about and now and then she would glance up at the house, so there was no doubt as to her destination. Judy returned her gaze to her husband. He seemed totally absorbed in the figure approaching them and, frowning, Judy said with unaccustomed sharpness,

'I asked you where the *Andromeda* was going!'

'Slowly he took his eyes off the girl in pink.

'The *Andromeda*?' he repeated absently. 'Oh ... to some of the islands, and to Egypt.'

'Egypt?' Her eyes glowed; she forgot the girl in her excitement. 'I've always wanted to go to Egypt. Can we go on the ship when she sails next month?'

'Together?' So soft the brief word ... and an odd expression in his eyes. Judy became guarded.

'Well, I could scarcely go on my own,' she evaded. 'It wouldn't be right, for one thing.' She was flushing and he smiled, but his manner of amused tolerance had vanished when he spoke.

'Whether it would be right or wrong is quite immaterial, Judy. The important thing is that I wouldn't allow you to go on your own.' He was all cool mastery, a husband whose word was law. Judy searched for something to say, but before any suitably impressive retort could be found Chris was speaking again, this time in affable, welcoming tones. 'Corinne, how nice to see you. You've been on the island some time?'

'A month.' Her brown eyes swept Judy an all-embracing glance. 'I sold four paintings, so I've used the money to come back. George was sweet; he rented me the room at the top of his house again.'

'Meet my wife, Judy. Judy dear, this is Corinne Moore, an artist friend of mine. She comes to Hydra to paint, then goes off somewhere to sell her work and returns just as soon as she can.'

Corinne ... the girl Chris had almost married! And if he had married her then she, Judy, would have been able to marry Ronnie.

'How do you do.' Corinne extended a hand and Judy took it. 'You didn't tell me you were engaged to a babe,' she laughingly said to Chris. 'How old is this child?'

Judy stiffened and her face went white. She hadn't

realized she had a temper until now. However, she restrained it with admirable calm as she said with feigned innocence,

'I shall be eighteen in two months' time—so I'm not really all that young. . . .' A subtle pause and then, slowly, 'But I expect it seems young to you, Miss Moore, for you must be nearing thirty.'

No one was more amazed at her words than Judy herself. Strictly brought up, with a strong adherence to good manners, she had never before insulted anyone, either knowingly or unknowingly. But the girl had asked for it, she told herself, watching the colour flood Corinne's cheeks. A little fearfully, Judy stole a glance at her husband. He was staring at her in astonishment, but there was a most odd light in his eye too . . . as if a sudden idea had just occurred to him. He said admonishingly,

'My dear, where are your manners? Corinne is an old friend of mine, and our guest.'

But an uninvited one, said Judy to herself, wondering why she should dislike the girl on sight. She did not want to apologize, but she felt ashamed of her lapse.

'I'm sorry,' she murmured with difficulty. 'I spoke without thinking.' Not exactly a gracious apology, but it was all the girl was going to receive.

Corinne looked at her through narrowed eyes. And she seemed to be endeavouring to convey the message that Judy would be well advised not to make an enemy of her. But Judy was fast gaining confidence in herself. She was no longer the little orphan who had fallen under her grandfather's stern control; she was a wife now, a wife whose intention it was to assert herself, whether it be with her husband, or her husband's ex-girl-friends.

CHAPTER FOUR

FLORIA arrived three days later and from the first there sprung up a friendship between the two girls. They swam together in the mornings when Chris was otherwise occupied; they strolled together down to the harbour or to the beach farther along where they would swim or just sit watching the glistening blue-green sea and talking. Judy had little to tell Floria because her life had been simple. She had been sent to a private school in Kyrenia which was run by an Englishwoman but where she had learned to speak the Greek language. From there she had gone to the *gymnasium*, the Greek name for a grammar school, and lastly she had been sent by her grandfather to the school in France. A few months later she was married, and at that time she thought her life was finished, for the bottom seemed to have dropped out of her world when she realized she would never set eyes on Ronnie again. But somehow she was not nearly so heartbroken as she expected to be, nor did she dislike her husband as she had expected to dislike him. Perhaps that was because he was so docile and easily managed. She had expected to be domineered and subdued, to be a slave to her husband's fancies and whims. She had resigned herself to her husband's indifference and to his eventual infidelity, for this was the lot of the majority of the girls she knew. But she had discovered she had courage; she had also been fortunate in having Lefki for a friend, and that had made all the diifference.

'Tell me about yourself now,' she urged as she and Floria sat on the beach. 'I've told you my life story in less than five minutes,' she added, laughing.

'Mine can be told in less than that, even. Like you, I attended a private school. But I wasn't fortunate enough to go to France like you. My father's old-fashioned when it comes to girls being educated. Chris went to the university in Athens. It wasn't fair.'

'Are you glad you're married?' Judy was instantly sorry she had phrased the question, for a dark, brooding expression entered Floria's eyes.

'I don't know. . . . I suppose Vincent is, on the whole, a good man.'

A good man? Judy frowned. Was Floria unhappy? In saying Vincent was a good man she merely followed the pattern. A wife would refer to her husband as a good man, a husband would refer to his wife as a good woman. Never a reference to the vital quality of love. It was not expected by either side.

'Vincent's coming here soon—that's what Chris said '

Floria nodded, her brooding gaze on the sea.

'In about a week.'

'What's he like?' Judy wanted to know, drawing her knees up under her chin. Both girls were in shorts and sun-tops, and both possessed a lovely golden tan which was the envy of the tourists who flocked from the cruise ships and ferries on to the island for a couple of hours or so before boarding the ship again and making for yet another Greek island.

'Vincent?' Floria brought her gaze from the sea and turned to look at Judy. 'Small, and stout and dark——' She shrugged. 'Nothing glamorous about him like Chris. You're lucky, Judy. My brother's the handsomest man I've ever seen.' Judy said nothing. You weren't lucky if you had to marry someone you did not love—whether he happened to be handsome or not. 'He offered for you two years ago, didn't he? You'd only be fifteen?'

She nodded.

'Yes, I was.'

'Weren't you flattered?' The hint of envy in Floria's voice was not lost on Judy and she felt somehow that her husband's sister would rather not be married.

'I wasn't flattered, no,' she replied truthfully. 'I didn't want to be engaged at that age. My grandfather made me, though, so I had no choice.'

'You're glad now, though?' Floria gave her a curious glance before turning her face to the sea again.

'I didn't want to marry Chris,' she owned after a moment's hesitation, and her sister-in-law gave a start of amazement.

'You didn't? But why?'

Judy shrugged. She could not tell Floria that she loved someone else, so she merely said she felt she was too young to marry.

'If men can wait until they're nearly thirty, then why can't women?' she went on to add.

'I wouldn't like to wait that long.' But a small sigh left Floria's lips and again Judy felt that she would prefer not to be married. For some reason Judy said,

'You're happy with Vincent?'

A long pause and then,

'I love someone else,' admitted Floria, her voice husky and low. 'And I think he would have come to love me if only my father had not forced me into marriage with Vincent.'

'He doesn't love you at present, then?'

Floria shook her head.

'If he had loved me he'd have offered, wouldn't he?'

Judy gave a helpless little gesture with her hands.

'They offer when they don't love you—so you don't really know where you are.'

Floria smiled then, in some amusement.

'You sound as if you don't care very much for men.'

She did care for one man.... What was Ronnie doing now? Perhaps already he had found someone else—a girl unhampered by custom, an English girl who could marry him. Pain caught at her heart for a moment, but it was gone before she could feel any degree of pity for herself. She was being remarkably brave, she told herself. To put Ronnie from her like this was a most praiseworthy achievement.

'I don't dislike men, not really,' said Judy at last. 'It's just that I think it most unfair that they get such a better deal than women.'

'In the East they do, but not in the West. I wish I'd been born in the West.'

'It didn't do me much good——' Appalled, Judy broke off. But it was too late. Floria brought her gaze from the sea to stare at Judy incredulously.

'You sound as if you actually hate being married to my brother!' she exclaimed on an incredulous note. 'Do you dislike him?'

'No, of course not,' Judy replied hastily. 'I only meant that, in my case, being British did not mean that I could choose my own husband, as would have been the case had my parents lived and I'd been brought up in my own country.' She felt disloyal to Chris, and guilty—but why? He had no right to offer for her when she was so young.

'I should have thought you would consider Cyprus as your own country. Also, you needn't have married Chris if you really hadn't wanted to. From things you've said your grandfather was kind, and he allowed for the fact that your father was English. I met him once, remember?—and I gained the impression then that he would always consider your happiness before anything else.' Floria paused, her eyes still on Judy. 'I think you really wanted to marry Chris, because if you

71

hadn't you'd have put up a fight—and you would have won.'

The protest that rose to Judy's lips was suddenly checked. She found herself reflecting on her sister-in-law's pronouncement that she, Judy, had really wanted to marry Chris. But she hadn't, Judy told herself emphatically. Of course she hadn't wanted to marry Chris. The very idea was ridiculous, simply because it was Ronnie she had loved. Judy's brow creased in a frown. Before she had met Ronnie ... what were her feelings towards the marriage? She had been resigned, she had asserted on her grandfather's bringing the matter up.... But was it resignation? Hadn't she told Lefki—not without a hint of pride—that Chris was far more handsome than Paul? And hadn't she rather enjoyed dancing with him at Margarita's wedding? Could these things possibly mean that she had subconsciously found Chris attractive, and that was why she had never put forward any protest until she eventually realized it was Ronnie she wanted to marry?

At this point in her musings Judy's thoughts became troublesome and bewildering. Had she really been in love with Ronnie? There was no doubt at all that she had put him out of her mind with more ease than she would ever have thought possible, and on the rare occasions when he did intrude, his features were somewhat blurred and elusive. Impatient with her inability either to admit or deny the truth of Floria's assertion, Judy dismissed the matter altogether and made to change the subject, intending to ask Floria about this man whom she loved, but then she checked her words, realizing that it was not quite the thing to do. In any case, Floria spoke, asking in the most matter-of-fact way if Judy had met Corinne Moore yet.

'She's staying up at George Cozakis's place,' Floria added. 'Has a studio in the roof—an odd sort of character she is.'

'I've met her once.' Judy's tones were stiff and cold.

'I suppose you know she's in love with Chris?' Floria's tones were still matter-of-fact. So many girls had been in love with her brother.

'George said they were nearly married,' began Judy when she was interrupted by her sister-in-law.

'He exaggerates.' She stopped, puzzling Judy by the sudden flush that tinged her cheeks. But a moment later she went on, 'They were—er—more than friends, but there never was any question of marriage. If Corinne had played her cards right I do believe there would have been a chance for her, but it developed into an affair, and Chris would never marry a girl like that.'

Judy swallowed. Why should she care that Chris and Corinne had had an affair?

'You mean ... if Corinne had not let——? What I'm trying to say is ...' Her voice trailed away into silence and a deep flush spread over her cheeks. To her surprise Floria laughed and said with complete lack of embarrassment,

'If Corinne had not let Chris have all he wanted she might have led him very nicely into marriage, for there's no doubt that she had an enormous attraction for him—none of the others were in his favour for so long.'

A soft breeze blew across the sea, and Judy was more than a little thankful for its cooling effect on her hot face.

'How long was she—er—in his favour?' she could not help asking.

'Now let me see. ... It's about four years since he first met her. She came here to paint, and was looking for somewhere to live. Chris had a villa by the harbour and she came up here to see if he would let it to her, but it was already let on a long lease to an American family who come every summer for three months. Chris did find her a flat, however, but of course she couldn't afford to live on the island all the time and she went off to England or somewhere to find a job. When she came back the following summer the flat was let to someone else and George let her have a room in his house. She's come here quite often since then because he doesn't charge her anything, her being a friend of Chris—and Chris being a friend of George, if you know what I mean?'

'So she and Chris have been friends for about four years—on and off?' Judy waited, all cold and stiff inside at the idea that Chris should be having an affair with Corinne while engaged to Judy herself. Men were horrid creatures, she thought, and wished her new-found courage had come to her earlier so that she could have thrown him over! How surprised he would have been! And there would never have occurred that scene over her friendship with Ronnie. Just to think, Chris had told her grandfather that, had he thought she had done any real wrong, he would not be wanting to marry her. And he himself had had scores of women— and one woman in particular ... Corinne Moore.

'Yes, it's at least four years.' A small pause and then, 'She was dreadfully upset when he told her he was engaged to you——'

'He told her right away?' Judy knew he must have informed Corinne that he was engaged, because she had mentioned it herself when asking her age, but somehow Judy would not have expected him to tell the girl until just before the marriage.

'Yes, he told her as soon as he came back from Cyprus. She didn't speak to him for weeks, but then she came round again and they used to go off to Athens for week-ends.'

Judy drew a deep breath, endeavouring to release the tightness in her throat. How utterly disgusting for him to go off for week-ends—— She checked her angry thoughts. After all, such behaviour was not by any means unusual. Chris had been forced to wait two years for her and she knew full well that he would find pleasure in the meantime.

Why had he married her? Judy then asked herself. Surely, as Corinne was so attractive to him, it would have been more enjoyable to continue in that sort of relationship indefinitely. Or he could have married Corinne, even though they had been lovers. But no, Floria was right when she said Chris would never marry a woman like that. Greeks very rarely did marry their lovers; they invariably chose an innocent young girl for a wife. And what of Chris's life now? Judy knew a moment of fear. Would he return to Corinne because she, Judy, would not allow him to make love to her?

'Oh dear,' she whispered fearfully. 'Perhaps I've made a mistake.' Should she tell him she had changed her mind? Judy blushed at the idea of that. Besides, they had been married little over a week; they were still strangers, with no affection between them yet. No, she must wait a little while until they knew each other better.

On the way back they met George, walking along the quay. He smiled at the two girls and fell into step beside them.

'Two lovely girls without their men,' he said teasingly. 'I'm certainly in luck!'

Floria looked down at her feet, avoiding his gaze. Judy's eyes flickered as she watched her. Could it be that she did not like George...? Suddenly Judy recalled that blush when she spoke about him a few minutes ago on the beach, and all at once she felt that

George was the man Floria loved. Her heart went out to her and a great sigh left her lips. How sad it all was! Floria married to Vincent, whom she did not love, while here was George, so handsome and charming and gay. . . . But he did not appear to be in any way attracted to Floria, and it did seem that Floria had been indulging in fanciful ideas when she had said he would have come to love her had her father not forced her into marriage with Vincent.

They came to the *taverna*, set back from the harbour and shaded by trees and an abundance of hibiscus and oleanders and other exotic flowering bushes. George suggested that they have something to drink, making his way to the *taverna* even as he spoke.

They sat in the shade drinking iced orange and watching the life going on around them. Men playing cards at a nearby table, a white donkey loaded with the luggage of a young couple who had just come off the ferry from Piræus. They were coming to the island for a lengthy stay, judging by the amount of luggage they had brought with them. They looked English, or American, Judy concluded, and drew George's attention to them.

'Mr. and Mrs. Palmer, from New York City. They come every year about this time. Mr. Palmer's the principal of a college there, and his wife's a private nurse. They must get devilish high salaries in America, because they come here for about ten weeks.'

'They'd have to live at home, though,' Judy pointed out. 'And it might be much cheaper to live here than in New York City.'

'The actual living undoubtedly is,' he readily agreed. 'But what about the fares? In any case, they don't stay on Hydra all the time; they'll be tripping off to Athens or Delphi or to one or other of the islands.' They had seen him and they told the man leading the donkey to wait. 'Back again already?' said George, standing up to give Mrs. Palmer his seat. 'It seems like a couple of months ago since you were here.'

'Time goes far too quickly. No, George, we won't sit down, but thanks all the same. We want to get settled in and then we can relax and do all the things one should do on holiday.'

'You must dine with me quite soon. I'll arrange a party.'

'Thanks a lot, George; we'll look forward to that.' Mr. Palmer looked at the two girls and George made the introductions.

'Chris's new wife!' exclaimed Mrs. Palmer. 'But how nice to meet you, dear. He told us he was engaged, but that you were too young. Lucky girl! He must have loved you to wait all this time—two years or more, I guess it must have been. Well, we'll be seeing you around. Goodbye for now.' And they went on their way, to the grey house on the hillside which had been let to them regularly each summer for the past seven years.

He must have loved you. What silly things some people did say! But then Mrs. Palmer was an American, and in America they married for love.

By the end of the following week both Chris's mother and Vincent had arrived at Salaris House. Madam Voulis greeted Judy with a smile and a kiss; she fully approved her son's choice and let both Chris and Judy see it.

'You look glowing, my dear,' she declared effusively. 'Marriage agrees with you, obviously.'

That startled Judy. With uneasy reluctance she cast a glance at her husband from under her lashes. He cocked an eyebrow, but it was his rather dry expression that disconcerted her and the colour leapt to her face.

77

'Marriage and this lovely island,' put in Vincent, relaxing in his chair. He was dark and stout and oily. Judy glanced across at Floria, sitting upright on a high-backed chair, small and dainty and wistful. Judy thought of George and a sadness crept over her. George and Floria would have made a well-matched pair.... But what was the use of dwelling on that? Floria was married to Vincent, and there could be no other future for her but that of his wife.

'You like it here?' Madam Voulis's eyes were fixed admiringly on her daughter-in-law, taking in every lovely curve of her face and neck and shoulders. For Judy was wearing a brief sun-suit—all too revealing, she had protested when Chris had told her to put it on. He himself had bought it in Athens, where he had been for two days last week, on business. There had been a tussle over the sun-suit, and Judy had been defeated, much to her consternation, because it seemed to prove that Chris was quite able to master her if he so desired. Deeply troubled by what appeared to be a set-back, Judy had written to her friend, tentatively asking Lefki what she would have done under the circumstances.

'Yes, I like it very much,' she said in reply to Madam Voulis's question.

'Better than Cyprus?' Vincent thrust his hands deeply into his pockets and stretched his legs out in front of him.

'Naturally I like Cyprus better,' said Judy with a frown. He was slothful, she thought, and wondered if he had money of his own or whether it was Floria's dowry that kept him in idleness. His eyes were roving lasciviously over her and Judy became aware of the swift compression of her husband's lips.

'If we're not doing any more sunbathing you can go and change,' he snapped, turning to his wife. Her chin

78

lifted at his order; he himself had made her put the suit on and he must have known that any man who happened to see her would stare. But it appeared it was only Vincent to whom he objected, and Judy could not help wondering if Chris did not altogether trust his sister's husband.

'We might go out again shortly,' she began, feeling she must make a stand. 'I'll change later——'

'You'll change now.' Slow and deliberate the words; Judy flushed because all eyes were on her. She left the room without further argument, but as she passed her husband she lifted her head and glared at him. He set his lips again, but she was gone before he could speak.

Several days passed, lazily and pleasantly, for all of them were in a holiday mood. Judy and Floria visited the Palmers one morning and they all went down to the swimming pool. George had arranged his dinner party and they were all invited, so on parting just before lunch time they said they would be meeting again that evening.

'So long, girls,' said Mrs. Palmer gaily when, on reaching a fork in the narrow twisting lane going up into the hillside, they went their separate ways. 'Be good!'

'Be good,' repeated Floria disgustedly. 'How can a girl be anything else here!'

Turning, Judy stared.

'Do you want to be anything else?' she asked with a half laugh.

'I think it would be fun to have an affair.'

'You don't!' Judy declared emphatically, shocked.

'Men have affairs, so why can't we?'

For a moment Judy said nothing. Like Floria she considered it most unfair that men could enjoy total freedom while women must carry discretion to ridiculous limits. Nevertheless, she herself had no desire to

79

indulge in an affair—no, not even with Ronnie, whom she had dearly loved.

'With women, it isn't the done thing,' answered Judy unnecessarily. 'We'd be disgraced for ever.'

'I sometimes think I wouldn't care.' They were climbing steeply, taking step after step up the lane. Houses on both sides gleamed, white and blue, while on the steps leading up to the front doors were pots of gay flowers—modest roses and carnations. And there was the more flamboyant hibiscus with its huge scarlet trumpets. These bushes grew up the sides of the houses, contrasting vividly with the brilliant whiteness of the walls. Bougainvillea sprayed the cobblestones with violet petals that came drifting down incessantly, carried by the breeze sweeping gently down from the high places. Exotic perfumes filled the air. Paradise Isle, this rock had been called, and Judy felt its romance as one would feel the romance of a promised land. Some magical power seemed suddenly to hold her poised in space, in timeless space, vast and bewildering and enticing. Something within this vast eternity of space seemed to beckon, but from what direction she did not know. She was entranced and floundering, spellbound and excited, groping and sinking all at once.

Swiftly she turned, her spine tingling.

'Chris!' she exclaimed. 'How long have you been following us?'

Falling into step beside her, he regarded her searchingly from his superior height.

'You're not overjoyed at my appearance,' he commented drily, taking the next couple of steps in one languid stride. 'Do I intrude into maidens' secrets?'

'We were talking,' put in Floria unexpectedly, 'about the unfairness of men being able to indulge in affairs while women can't.'

Judy held her breath, peeping up at Chris in a

rather horrified sort of way. To her surprise he asked calmly,

'Does one of you desire to indulge in an affair?'

'Oh no, Chris,' returned his wife hastily. 'We were only talking about the unfairness, as Floria has just remarked.' Why was she so breathless at the sight of her husband? He had said she was not overjoyed at his appearance, and of course that was true ... and yet how must she account for the sudden jerking of her heart as she turned to find him walking there? More important, how must she account for the prior knowledge that he was near? For she did know he was near....

'Tell me honestly, Chris,' said his sister as they turned in preparation to take the last flight of steps up to the house, 'do you consider it unfair?'

'Unfair?' He transferred his gaze from his wife to his sister, giving her a mild stare. 'I don't know what you're talking about, Floria.'

'You do!' She actually stamped her foot. 'Why can't women have affairs?'

The deceptive cool disinterest vanished. Chris's dark eyes glinted.

'You talk like a baggage,' he snapped, then added, 'If the matter is so vital, then I suggest you discuss it with your husband.'

Floria bent her head, but not before Judy had noted the swiftly rising colour and the sharp catching of her lips between her teeth. It was George with whom she desired to have an affair, obviously, but it was also obvious that Floria was exceedingly afraid of her husband, for at the very mention of him just now she had seemed to tremble. She had of course started all wrong, decided Judy knowledgeably. Pity she hadn't had a friend like Lefki who would have taught her a thing or two. But of course there wasn't another like Lefki—she

81

was unique among women in this part of the world.

On their arrival at the house Floria went inside while Chris and Judy stayed on the verandah for a few minutes while waiting for lunch to be served.

'What's all this nonsense about affairs?' Chris asked abruptly the moment they sat down. 'It's disgusting talk for two young married women!'

He sounded angry, she thought, recalling that she had seen him angry only once before—when he had tackled her about meeting Ronnie. That was more than anger, she mused, feeling again that grip on her wrist and seeing the dark fury in his eyes. He had reduced her to a jelly, so afraid of him she had been. That was before she gained courage, though. He would not be able to terrify her so easily now.

'The conversation just drifted in that direction,' she murmured after a little hesitation.

'There must have been some reason for this "drifting" as you term it.'

Was it a question? Her husband's mouth was set, his eyes narrowed and coldly metallic. This was somehow like an entirely new man, someone she did not know. She had become used to his mild tolerance alternating with indifference. He had asked her questions before, but evasion on her part had resulted in a bored dismissal of the topic and Judy had been left with the impression that he had not really been interested in receiving answers to his questions at all.

But now his attitude was demanding and stern.

'I can't think how it all began,' she said at last. 'Perhaps it was because of what Mrs. Palmer said.'

'Jean Palmer? What did she say?'

Judy gave a little shrug, feeling foolish as she answered,

'She said "be good".'

Chris stared at her, as well he might.

'Be more explicit,' he ordered at last. 'Why were you and Floria talking about women having affairs?'

Unable to repeat what Floria had said about thinking it would be fun to have an affair, Judy said with a tinge of apprehension,

'I don't know how to answer you, Chris. It was a—a private conversation——'

'And an incriminating one,' he broke in swiftly. 'Obviously Floria is discontented with her life——'

'Anyone would be discontented with Vincent,' Judy had flashed before she could check herself.

An arrogant gleam entered her husband's eyes. His voice was steel as he said,

'A woman should be satisfied with her husband, no matter what he's like. Has she been speaking to you about Vincent in disparaging terms?' he wanted to know after a small pause.

Vigorously she shook her head.

'No, honestly.' But although she had not lied Judy knew she had left the important thing unsaid and she felt the colour rise in her cheeks. Chris kept his gaze upon her, his unmoving countenance causing her a tinge of fear in spite of her good resolutions and firm decision not to allow him to frighten her again.

'Is Floria in love with someone?' inquired Chris at last, and Judy's eyes flew to his. This was all he required, but even as she saw perception dawn the other aspect of his words impressed itself on her mind. 'Is Floria in love with someone?' . . . not someone *else*.

'So you know she's not in love with Vincent?' she said, half hoping to divert him until the gong should call them to lunch, bringing an end to this most uncomfortable conversation.

'Of course she's not in love with Vincent. It was an arranged marriage like that of everyone else. Who is this man with whom she desires to have an affair?' he demanded to know, but Judy shook her head, looking him directly in the eye this time.

'I don't know, Chris——'

'So she does want to have an affair? he broke in, and Judy put a nervous hand to her head.

'You're tying me up in knots,' she complained. 'I shouldn't have said that. Floria's affairs are her own and she'll be so angry at my slip. Please don't tell her, or be angry with her,' she pleaded, looking at him with a troubled gaze. 'I don't know if she does want to have an affair.' She stopped, reluctant to say more because her suspicions were strong within her and should her husband persist in questioning her about this man with whom Floria was in love she might inadvertently reveal those suspicions. And that would be disastrous, for George was not only a friend of Chris but also a close business associate. 'You won't say anything to Floria?' she asked again, drawing a deep breath as the gong sounded at last.

He stood up, and with an unexpected gesture reached down and pulled Judy up beside him.

'It's not my business,' he said at length. 'Let her husband deal with the problem. He'll probably beat her——'

'Oh no!' cut in Judy, appalled at the idea. 'He wouldn't do that, surely?' She was looking up at Chris, her blue eyes scared and her lips quivering. After regarding her in silence for a moment Chris suddenly took her chin in his hand and, before she could grasp his intention, he had kissed her full on the mouth.

'Certainly he would,' he answered unemotionally, and paused a little while, again looking into her face. Could he sense the queer little rhythm of her heartbeats? she wondered, profoundly stirred because the warmth of his kiss still remained on her lips. 'Certainly he would,' repeated Chris, and then, deliberately, and

84

very softly, 'So would any husband worth his salt …
even if his wife only looked at another man, let alone
harboured thoughts of having an affair with him.' He
kissed her again, possessively. She would have liked to
draw away because the kiss was not at all like Ronnie's,
and it scared her a little. But a warning voice told her
not to draw away … and just as Chris stopped kissing
her she made the disturbing and quite incredible discovery that she would have liked to respond to his kiss,
and that she felt somewhat flat because it was now too
late. Her beautiful eyes were raised to his; he smiled
down at her, but his eyes were metal. 'So take care,' he
warned, and strode briskly away in the direction of the
house.

CHAPTER FIVE

THAT evening they all set out together to go to George's party. Vincent, declaring that he could not walk so great a distance, rode on a white donkey, much to Judy's disgust, for one could never get the smell of the animal off one's clothes. Vincent did not appear to care; in any case, he had not troubled to acquire the immaculate appearance of Chris, although his pretty wife had taken great care to look her best. Judy was in lilac, with a matching ribbon in her hair; it made her look younger than her age, she knew, and when Chris shook his head, after allowing his eyes to flicker over her from head to foot, she was well aware that he was once again seeing her as a child.

To Judy's dismay Corinne Moore was invited to the dinner party—and Judy did wonder how she could have forgotten she was staying in George's house and, therefore, would naturally be his guest this evening. She looked dazzling in blue, the neck of her dress so low it left nothing to the imagination. Her dark hair shone, and it flowed in waves on to her shoulders . . . the sort of hair a man would want to bury his face in, Judy admitted grudgingly. Long dark lashes threw shadows on to sun-tanned cheeks; the brown eyes were liquid and alive. No doubt about it, Corinne Moore was devastatingly attractive. And she had the assurance of a woman of the world in addition to possessing the ability to use the charms nature had so lavishly bestowed upon her.

Judy felt like a tiny star outshone by a glowing silver moon.

Corinne sat opposite to Chris at the table, which was lit with candles, the electric lights in the room having been switched off. It was a romantic atmosphere, with the soft lights and music in the background. Corinne monopolized Chris, and once or twice Judy caught George looking strangely at them and then transferring his gaze to herself. Two things Judy learned even before the meal was over: Corinne Moore was in love with Chris, and Floria definitely was in love with George. What of George's feelings for Floria? He spoke to her often, but impersonally. This was not a pointer to his feelings, decided Judy. He could scarcely be anything other than impersonal in the presence of both Floria's husband and her brother. Another thing Judy learned that night: Chris had no idea that George was the man Floria loved.

Vincent talked a good deal to Judy, and always she was uncomfortably aware of what could only be described as a leering gaze fixed on her the whole time. And when, the meal over, they all went out on to the softly lighted patio, Vincent somehow managed to seat himself beside his sister-in-law. His arms slid across the top of her chair and then dropped on to her shoulder. She looked round for her husband and discovered that he was missing. And so was Corinne ... they were at the far end of the patio, she presently discovered, practically hidden by the vines and the oleander bushes. The temper Judy had discovered she possessed suddenly flared, but she had of course to control it, there being no one on whom she could vent it. But wait until she was home again ... and alone with her husband!

'What are you drinking, Judy?' George's voice cut into her angry musings and she managed to smile. She told him what she wanted and he poured it for her, clinking his own glass against hers a moment later and sitting down at the other side of her. The night was warm and sultry, the air filled with heady perfumes and the sound of crickets and the occasional sheep bell or bray of a donkey on the lonely hillside. 'Just look at the lights of that ship out there——' George pointed seawards to where the lights of a pleasure cruiser gleamed above the horizon. 'It's probably one of ours.'

'Will it be?' Judy edged forward on her seat, trying to free herself from the clammy touch of Vincent's hand on her shoulder.

George nodded.

'Could be; we have a fleet of pleasure ships all over the seas round here at present.'

'There's a new one being launched, I heard you telling Chris?'

'That's right. She's a beauty——' He broke off, and then, as if making a decision, 'Would you like to see the plan of the *Andromeda*?' he asked eagerly. 'I don't suppose Chris has shown it to you; he isn't that interested, but I am. You see, I've not been with the firm that long. Do you want to see the plan?' he asked again.

She did, if only to get away from Vincent.

'Now where are you off to?' asked Jean Palmer as Judy and George rose from their chairs. Jean spoke banteringly, but she was a loud-voiced woman and her words carried to the two at the far end of the patio. Judy was conscious of her husband's attention being diverted from his glamorous companion to herself, but she was unable to read his expression owing to the distance and the foliage. 'This place is far too romantic,' Jean was saying, while her husband laughed loudly. 'You'll be getting up to something out there in the moonlit garden.'

George laughed; Floria, who had been deep in conversation with her mother, glanced up quickly on hearing Jean's question and her eyes rested first on George and then on Judy.

'We're not going into the garden,' George informed Jean. 'We're going into the house to see——'

'That's worse,' put in Keith Palmer. 'George, I know you of old. You want watching! Chris, what are you doing allowing your new wife to go off in the dark with your best friend?' It was all very lighthearted, but suddenly a tenseness enveloped them all except the Palmers, who sat there laughing and uttering further teasing remarks to no one in particular.

'Come on,' said George, rather sharply. 'Take no notice of these two!' And when they had entered the house and he had switched on the light in his study he added, 'That was in extremely bad taste.'

'They were only joking.'

'Obviously—but talk like that can cause trouble.'

'Trouble?' She went over to the massive desk and stood looking across the room at him. 'What do you mean, George?'

Colour had entered his face; he seemed unable to supply an answer, but Judy wanted one and she repeated her question.

'Remarks like that put odd thoughts into people's minds,' he said after a long and silent pause.

'What kind of odd thoughts? And who are the people to whom you refer?'

'Oh ... let it drop,' he returned, again with a sharp edge to his voice. And then he added, on noting Judy's expression, 'I'm sorry. That was downright rude of me.' His nerves seemed to be on edge and her eyes glinted perceptively. He had been thinking of Floria.... And that could only mean that he cared for her.

What a damnable situation. George and Floria in love—and Floria married to that horrid Vincent, married to him by the order of her father. Her father.... What was he like? No one ever mentioned him, and all at once it struck Judy that this unknown man was her father-in-law. Did he know he had a new relative? It was unlikely—unless Chris had written to him. He lived in Sparta, that much Judy did know, for her grandfather had mentioned it once.

'Is that the plan?' asked Judy, pointing to the wall, and anxious to put George at his ease because at the moment he was looking extremely apologetic and uncomfortable.

'No, I have it here.' Opening a drawer in his desk, he withdrew the rolled-up plan. Together they spread it out on the desk and leant over it. The various decks were described to Judy, and George pointed out the two swimming pools and the sports deck.

'There are two night clubs, a theatre—that's here,' he added, pointing to it. 'There's a nursery, and a playroom for the children. And the cabins are just marvellous. I must go to Venice and see it set sail on its first voyage,' he said with ever-increasing enthusiasm. 'I only wish I could take the cruise.'

'It's certainly a beautiful ship.' Judy spent some silent minutes looking at the plan. The *Andromeda* must surely be one of the most luxurious cruise ships sailing the Mediterranean. 'I asked Chris to take me on the cruise,' she told George. 'It calls at Egypt—at Alexandria—and I've always wanted to go there. I want to see the Pyramids and the Sphinx. But Chris didn't reach any decision,' she added.

'You mean he was considering going?' asked George in surprise.

'Not really. I was asking Chris about the cruise, but before we could discuss it properly Corinne came and interrupted us. I mentioned it again a few days later, but Chris was busy and wouldn't listen. I never mentioned it again because I thought it would be too late. It sails next week, doesn't it?'

'That's right—on Sunday from Venice, as I said.' He paused in thought. 'It would be a wonderful trip for you, Judy.' He smiled at her and added, 'You haven't had a honeymoon, have you? There might be a cabin vacant—I could find out—and if so Chris might take you.'

A cabin. . . . Softly the colour fused her cheeks. On asking Chris to take her she had concluded that they would have separate cabins. But then Chris had murmured that one subtle word 'together' and she had suddenly become guarded. However, even then she had not been unduly worried. She had told him right at the start that they must keep company and get to know each other better before she allowed him to be her real husband. Her word was still law about that and Chris was apparently fully resigned to this fact.

George was poring over the plan again, pointing out things he had missed, but Judy's thoughts were now entirely on her husband. Were they getting to know one another better? Chris was so aloof and more often than not quite unapproachable. Sometimes it would seem that he did not have the least desire to know her better, and this was most odd indeed, seeing that he had married her for desire alone and the sooner they did get to know one another the sooner his desire would be fulfilled. Judy reached the conclusion that there was something inexplicable about the whole aspect of their relationship and wondered why it had not struck her before now.

It would almost seem that, having married her, he had then decided he did not really want her after all. Could that be the reason why Chris had appeared to bow so meekly to her will? Could it be that she had been giving herself a pat on the back for nothing?— that she was not being clever at man-management at all, but that she had appeared to succeed simply because Chris no longer desired her? Certainly she had many times pondered over this meekness of his, for undoubtedly he was a man of strong personality, and she was sure that had he the mind he could bend her to his will, no matter what Lefki said about all men being the same.

A tight little lump gathered in Judy's throat and she suddenly wanted to cry. If all her plans had gone wrong—and she now felt sure they had—then how could their marriage succeed? She had certainly wanted it to succeed, stoically making herself forget Ronnie, whom she had loved to desperation, and waiting for the time when some affection would grow up between Chris and herself so that they could be happy together, like Lefki and Paul. Yes, that was what Judy had been aiming for—a marriage as successful as her friend's, where she herself would be her husband's equal and mutual respect would play its all-important part in their relationship. Anger against her husband rose up to take the place of her desolation. He had no right to marry her and then not want her! That she was being somewhat illogical did not strike her as she continued silently to condemn him. He should have left her alone to marry the man she loved; he should have stayed with Corinne—— Corinne! So *that* was why he did not want his wife. Judy had already wondered if he would return to Corinne.

'Oh . . .' she breathed. 'I hate him!'

'What did you say?' George looked up from his concentrated perusal of the plan. Judy flushed a deep rosy red. She had forgotten all about George.

'Nothing,' she answered, feeling extremely foolish even though it was plain from her companion's expression that he had not heard her exact words. 'I was thinking aloud.'

'Obviously you were thinking aloud.' He straightened up and stared at her flushed face; Judy lowered her lashes because of the brightness of her eyes. But the tears were pricking her lids and she failed to hold them back. George just stood there, consternation spreading over his handsome face as she wept as if her heart would break. And then he came to life and took her gently in his arms so that she had the comfort of a shoulder to weep upon.

'Judy, whatever is the matter?' he asked perturbedly. 'Why are you crying like this?' His tones were gruff and hesitant; he was disconcerted, not knowing how to deal with the situation.

And Judy did not know how to answer, because she was not sure as to the real reason for her tears. Perhaps it was because of Ronnie, or simply that she was a little tired.... Judy would never own even to herself that her unhappiness stemmed from the discovery she had just made—that her husband no longer wanted her, but chose to find pleasure with Corinne instead.

George was giving her his handkerchief, and holding her away from him, gazing interrogatingly at her. What must she say to him? Her eyes fell on the plan....

'It's because I want to go on the cruise,' she said, grabbing the handkerchief and pressing it to her eyes, more to hide their expression than to dry her tears. 'And—and Chris won't take me.'

'He's a busy man, Judy——'

'He's on holiday now, and will be for the whole of the summer. He could take me.'

'Yes ... I suppose so, but——'

'What,' rasped a voice from the doorway, 'is going on here?'

'Chris!' Judy leapt away from George and pushed the handkerchief into her eyes again. 'We—we were looking at the plan of the *Andromeda*.'

His level gaze rested on her tear-stained face; she

93

noted the slight movement of a muscle in his neck and wondered fearfully if anger had caused it.

'Looking at a plan of the ship, were you?'. He directed the question at George, from whom he appeared to expect an explanation.

'That was the reason we came in here,' returned George, looking at Chris with an odd expression. 'I wanted to show the plan to Judy.'

'I see. And do you have to hold her in your arms in order to show her the plan?' A knife edge to his voice, dark fury glinting in his eyes. Judy looked apprehensively at him and then swiftly lowered her head.

'Chris,' said George, still eyeing his friend with that odd expression, 'don't get anything wrong. Judy was suddenly unhappy and I comforted her. It was an automatic gesture, I assure you.' The sincerity of his manner and the frankness of his gaze as he spoke to Chris, these were sufficiently impressive and Judy was relieved to see her husband's face begin to clear. But the movement in his throat continued and she watched it, fascinated and puzzled.

'I think,' said Chris abruptly, 'that I'd better take you home.' He turned to George. 'You'll excuse us?'

'Certainly.' A small pause and then, 'You know why Judy's unhappy? You heard?'

'I heard. Judy, go and collect your handbag, and everything else you left out there.' His curt order was obeyed without hesitation. Chris requested his friend to make their apologies, saying his wife was unwell, and very soon he and Judy were walking home in silence, each lost in thought.

Why had he left Corinne and come to find her? Judy asked herself. The feasible explanation was that he was annoyed at the remarks of the Palmers and this had led to pique that his wife should have gone off with George. But if Chris could occupy himself with

Corinne why shouldn't she, Judy, have similar freedom to occupy herself with George? This equality was what she was fighting for—and she was still determined to fight for equality even though all her plans for a happy marriage had crashed about her ears during those past few moments of enlightenment.

However, the more Judy dwelt on this feasible explanation the less it satisfied her, simply because it did not include the reason for Chris's decision to leave the party and take her home. She had been distressed and the natural thing for any husband would be to suggest that she go home, and that he accompany her—but that would be the situation only where a husband was concerned for his wife, and Chris was by no means concerned for his wife. In fact, for most of the evening he had been concerned with Corinne, and his action in deserting her, as it were, did not fit into Judy's neat little pattern at all, and once again she felt there was something inexplicable about Chris's attitude towards herself.

What were his own thoughts? she wondered, for he was so quiet—and sort of brooding. Was he thinking about the scene he had recently interrupted? Why hadn't he been angry about that? He had certainly been angry over Ronnie, she recalled with a slight shudder. Yet he had not believed her guilty of any real wrong—and he obviously did not take any great exception to the fact of her being in George's arms. Yes, there was indeed something inexplicable in her husband's attitude towards her, and suddenly she felt full, and choking inside, and a warmth spread through her because he trusted her.

She cast him an upward slanting look which brought a cool inscrutable response as Chris took his eyes off the bare rocky mass ahead, Mount Prophet Ilias, silhouetted against the dark mysterious reaches of an Eastern sky. She frowned, disliking intensely the look he gave her. It took him out of her world and placed him in some remote domain of his own, some lofty celestial realm where mere mortals such as she dare not tread. She had to break the silence, and a hint of irascibility edged her voice because there was something tantalizing about him ... and something profoundly disturbing.

'I'm sorry you had to come away from George's.' She didn't mean George, of course; she meant Corinne. Moreover, she wasn't sorry at all, on the contrary, she was glad that Corinne was now forced to make do with less attentive company, having been deprived of that of her lover.

'I didn't have to come away from George's,' was his mild rejoinder. He began walking more quickly, his long strides taking each step with ease as it came along. Judy had to trot; he must be aware of this, she thought, but it troubled him not at all.

'You had to take me home.' Her voice was sharp. She desired more than anything to lose her temper with him, but she was a trifle scared. He had treated that little scene all too calmly, she decided on recalling his barbed threat of what would happen to her if she only so much as looked at another man.

Dark frown lines creased her brow. Why should she allow herself to be scared? If Lefki had allowed herself to be scared she would never have won her fight for equality.

'I didn't have to take you home. I chose to do so.'
'Why?'
He subjected her to a frowning stare and said,
'What do you mean, why?'

She remembered her earlier anger at the attention he was extending to Corinne. She had determined to have it out with him about that and now she knew a sense of elation as her temper rose above her fear.

'Surely you would have preferred to stay with Corinne!'

To her surprise his lips twitched; he glanced perceptively at her. He appeared to be extraordinarily satisfied about something.

'So that troubled you, did it?' he commented with a dawning smile. 'Corinne is an old friend of mine, as you already know. I haven't seen her for a couple of months or so and therefore we were each catching up on the other's news.' His words were not an apology, but they *were* an explanation. She found it odd that he should take the trouble to offer her one and quite suddenly perceived that it was done deliberately.

He wanted to talk about Corinne! He might almost be trying to make her jealous, she thought, then dismissed the idea as ridiculous.

'I wasn't in the least troubled that you sat so long with Corinne,' she denied, but tartly. And with a daring born of her newly acquired courage she added, 'For my part, I was perfectly happy with George.'

Again that glance of perception, and accompanied by a deepening of his smile. What an enigma he was! She had expected anger, and another threat.... Another threat? Judy gasped, stunned by the revelation that she was thoroughly disappointed at not being threatened. What did it mean? She shook her head, bewildered. She had no wish to be threatened, she told herself crossly. She was striving for freedom, for equality—so how could she possibly want to be threatened?

'Happy, were you?' Amusement fringed his voice. 'Do you normally weep when you're happy?'

Her mouth compressed.

'I wanted to go on that cruise,' she said peevishly.

'So I believe,' yawned Chris. 'But why were you crying?'

'Because I wanted to go on the cruise. Why else should I be crying?' she added defiantly.

'That is what I'm trying to discover.'

Judy fell silent, disconcerted. She should have known he would not accept that as a reason for her tears; it was totally unconvincing. But to her surprise and relief he did not press her for a more likely explanation and they continued on their way to the house without another word passing between them. It was still early. The air was inexpressibly soft and clear, drenched with the timeless fragrance of oleanders growing along the dry river bed high on the hillside. On reaching the house Chris sat down in a low armchair on the patio. Automatically taking possession of the chair opposite to him, Judy picked up a magazine from the table and began idly to flick the pages, acutely aware of her husband's dark eyes fixed interestedly upon her.

'Do you really want to go on that cruise?' Reaching up, he snapped on the light. It was a soft amber, subdued and flattering to his wife's colouring and the burnished gold of her hair. She looked up; the pages of the book fluttered from her fingers as she stared at him, startled and disbelieving.

'You'll take me?' she quivered, conscious of the wild beating of her heart. Was it elation, because Chris was weakening and allowing her to have her own way? He was even willing to leave Corinne, it seemed, a circumstance which was puzzling in the extreme. 'Yes, indeed. I do want to go.'

Thoughtfully Chris watched her, leaning back in his chair, and Judy waited a little breathlessly for his decision.

'I'll find out tomorrow if there's any accommodation. There might not be, so don't built up your hopes.'

She wondered about the accommodation. But hadn't

she made her sentiments absolutely clear? And had not Chris meekly bowed to her will? Nevertheless, recalling again his subtle, softly spoken word 'together?' she found herself saying,

'Suppose they don't have enough cabins?'

'Enough?' He quirked an eyebrow and she blushed at the action. 'Do you mean two?' She could only nod and he said mockingly, 'So I must turn it down if there happens to be only one?'

She hesitated. From a small girl she had craved to visit Egypt.

'Perhaps—perhaps——' Judy coughed to clear her throat. 'What I mean to say is, it would be a shame if we had to miss the opportunity of going to Egypt simply because there was only one cabin.' Again she cleared her throat, disconcerted by his quizzical gaze. 'There might be two bunks in the cabin—if there happens to be only one cabin available, that is.' There were private bathrooms with many of the cabins, she recalled. The bathroom could serve as a dressing-room. She visualized no problems should they have to share a cabin.

Chris was leaning back in his chair, his long lean fingers tapping the arms as he watched Judy, his gaze still quizzical, yet narrowed with a degree of impatience.

'Your desire for a glimpse of Egypt is stronger than your fear of your husband, apparently,' was his sardonic comment at last.

Her chin lifted.

'Fear? I'm not afraid of you,' she swiftly let him know, wondering how he had managed to get an idea like that. She was standing up to him very well, and he knew it. To her surprise he laughed as if at some private joke of his own.

99

'Aren't you, Judy?' he inquired, rather gently, and her eyes flew to his.

'You know very well I'm not,' she returned with magnificent bravado, and then, with the uncomfortable conviction that he was enjoying himself at her expense, she changed the subject, reverting to the possibility of their taking the cruise. 'Do you think there will be some accommodation available?'

'I've just said, my dear, that I'll find out tomorrow.' Rising from his chair, he reached out and also brought Judy to her feet, his hold gentle on her wrist. 'I said it was going to be delightful being married to you—and I'm still of the same mind.' He was towering above her; she wondered why she trembled so and why she liked the nearness of him and the look in his eye and the way his hair came low on his forehead to form the 'V' of a widow's peak. And she did wonder too if he were aware of how profoundly she was affected by these things. All around them stillness hung in the perfumed air; they were enveloped in that magical, mothy darkness of a Grecian night. From the black mysterious hillside floated the tinkling sweetness of the sheep bells, and across the purple vault of the sky a star raced towards the dim horizon and was lost. Judy stirred beside her husband, caught in a web of timeless unreality, and completely detached from the world. There was no one in all this vast realm except her husband and herself. In the sweet intimacy of the moment he bent his head and kissed her, with gentle possessiveness and then with ardour, unfanned, restrained, but requiring little to coax it into an all-consuming flame. Of this Judy was sublimely unaware as she accepted his kiss, too shy and unsure of herself to respond. But she was warmed by his declaration that it was going to be delightful being married to her, for it revealed the fact that whatever he felt for Corinne it was not love. Judy's hopes for the future had been crushed earlier in the evening, but now they rose again. If she and Chris could go on that cruise together then they would surely get to know one another better, and that friendly relationship would develop into the affection which Judy desired to be established before she agreed to becoming a real wife to Chris.

And if affection did come to exist between Judy and her husband what price Corinne's designs then? A pleasant feeling of elation swept over Judy as, in thought, she had already ousted Corinne and taken her place in Chris's affections.

Chris had his cheek against Judy's hair, and then she felt the hardness of his lips on her temple. But when they found her mouth again they were soft and tender —and persuasive. She responded and felt a quiver run through him. Was it desire—or triumph? She drew away with more haste than diplomacy and half expected a quality of anger to replace the softness that had touched his face. Instead, he merely shook his head with the smallest hint of asperity and murmured across the space now dividing them,

'You're a tantalizing creature, Judy, and I only hope my patience lasts out.' He shook his head, as if he doubted that it would, and with a sudden frown Judy asked him what he meant. His eyes opened wide at this naïveté, but he saw at once that it was genuine and a softness marked his features again. 'Forget it, child. Just carry on as you are—you're doing very well,' he added with a smile of amusement not untinged with resignation.

Swiftly she glanced across at him, for in a flash of memory she recalled her slight suspicion that Chris had guessed what she was about. She said, taking a step towards him,

'Chris, why are you taking me to Egypt? Is it because

I wanted to go?'

His lips twitched, but his expression was wooden and his voice toneless as he answered,

'But of course. Why else?'

'You mean—that you've let me have my own way?'

'Isn't it apparent that I've let you have your own way?'

She frowned suspiciously at him. His dark face was still wooden.

'In England women have their own way. They're equals with their husbands.' That seemed irrelevant once it had been uttered, but Chris did not appear to notice.

'So I understand,' he returned with dry amusement.

Her suspicions remained. She wished she could understand this husband of hers. In appearance he was so superior and arrogant, and he was so muscular and strong. Surely he was aware that he could master her if he chose ... and yet he meekly accepted her decision over their marriage, and he had by his own admission let her have her own way regarding the projected cruise. It must be as Lefki said, men would capitulate rather than argue—if they were handled correctly, that was.

To her delight Chris managed to get two luxury cabins on the *Andromeda*, and there followed a flurry of preparation on Judy's part because the ship was sailing in five days' time. Floria's face took on an animated expression when Judy informed her that she and Chris were going on the cruise, and Judy regarded her with extreme puzzlement.

The reason for Floria's excitement was conveyed to Judy the same evening when, after dinner, when the family were sitting out as usual on the patio, Floria said to her brother,

'Can I come and see you off? I've always wanted to

see Venice.'

Chris frowned and directed his gaze to Floria's husband, slouched in a chair with a cigarette dangling between his lips and a string of worry beads clicking between his fingers. Vincent was going to Athens for a week, ostensibly on business, but Floria had recently confided to Judy that he had a woman friend there, an Englishwoman with whom he had been keeping company long before his marriage to Floria.

'I don't mind,' said Vincent in reply to his brother-in-law's unspoken question. 'I shan't be here anyway.'

'But she can't come back on her own.' Chris shook his head. 'No, Floria, it's impossible.'

Floria moistened her lips.

'George said something about going to see the *Andromeda* launched,' she remarked with a casualness that brought a tiny gasp of admiration from Judy, who by this time had the complete picture before her eyes. Floria could not have gone to Venice with George, but she could go with her brother and his wife. And as George would be returning there was no reason why Floria should not return with him.

'So he did.' Chris was thoughtful, considering, and Judy held her breath, saying a little prayer for her sister-in-law, yet wondering if the trip would eventually bring Floria more pain than pleasure. The Greek girl waited, tensed and pale, for her brother's verdict. Madam Voulis was also waiting, a slight frown between her eyes. Clearly she did not like the idea of Floria's going to Venice without her husband, but she voiced no protest, leaving the matter entirely to her son who, after what both to Judy and Floria seemed an eternity, said he would make up his mind after discussing the matter with George.

Judy, watching Floria, saw her face become even more pale and tensed. She was afraid her brother, after this consultation with George, would suspect the truth. But Judy had more faith in George than did Floria. She knew instinctively that he would successfully hide the truth from his friend. And he did. The following day Chris consented to Floria's accompanying Judy and himself to Venice, and later, when George dropped in for a drink, it was decided that the four of them should go to Venice on the day prior to the sailing.

'Seems a pity to go all that way and not even see the place,' commented George. 'I know you've been there, many times,' he went on to add, looking at Chris. 'But Judy hasn't and neither has Floria. If we go the day before we'll have a full twenty-four hours there, because embarkation isn't till five in the evening.'

'You're absolutely sure there's a flight back to Athens on the evening we sail?' inquired Chris of George.

He nodded.

'Yes, I'm quite sure, but, as I said, we'll have to stay overnight in Athens.'

'With your parents, you said? They can accommodate Floria?'

'Of course. Mother will be delighted to have the company.' He looked straight at Chris, and Judy glanced at Floria. The Greek girl was inexpressibly happy as she gazed back at her sister-in-law. Happy and innocent. In spite of what she had said about desiring to have an affair she *was* staying with George's parents.

CHAPTER SIX

THEY arrived in Venice at six in the evening and as they expected they had difficulty in obtaining rooms, it being the height of the season. No mention had previously been made between Judy and Chris regarding their accommodation in Venice, but Judy had somehow felt Chris would arrange for them to have separate rooms without the other two being aware of this.

However, when finally they did get fixed up, at one of the luxury hotels close to the Piazza San Marco, two rooms only were procurable. Chris came from the reception desk and glanced at his wife with a hint of mocking amusement as he said,

'Two rooms only, so you and Floria will have to share one, and George and I the other.'

'Oh,' said George, his eyes twinkling as he glanced from Chris to Judy and back again, 'what a shame. Only just married and separated so soon. Shall we try somewhere else?'

Judy flushed and lowered her head. Chris merely remarked that it was not important for one night and they were then shown up to their rooms. After dining at the hotel they went out into the *piazza*—the famous St. Mark's Square—and sat over cups of Venetian coffee and listened to the orchestra playing nostalgic, haunting music, while through the world's most glittering square sauntered a cosmopolitan crowd of tourists and natives. Cameras clicked at San Marco—surely the most photographed cathedral church in the world. Necks were craned as bedazzled eyes took in the spectacle of golden domes and crosses and the incredible campanile over three hundred feet high. The pavement of the square was of marble and trachyte; there were glittering mosaics and benches of pink marble. Over the whole magnificent square there was an atmosphere of gaiety and abandon; Judy was enthralled, her eyes shining like stars, her mouth slightly open as if she were breathing one long uninterrupted 'oh' of wonder and disbelief. Floria too was equally impressed. She had led an even more sheltered life than Judy, for she had never been out of her own country until now. Her pretty face glowed and, glancing at her, Judy surmised that this was the happiest occasion in the whole of Floria's life.

She and George were very discreet and Chris, sharp as he was, had no inkling of what went on beneath the surface. But Judy sensed the deep love which existed between these two and her heart ached for them. Her sadness clouded her eyes momentarily and, seeing this, her husband frowned and demanded to know what was wrong.

'Wrong?' Judy blinked at him uncomprehendingly.

'A moment ago you looked as if you were on top of the world, but now you appear to be in the depths of despair. What are you thinking about?'

Inadvertently she glanced from Floria to George and then with the swiftness of fear lest she had given something away she dropped her eyes.

'Nothing in particular,' she replied, and then added, in order to change the subject, 'This is a wonderful city, and I think I'm very lucky indeed to be here. It was kind of you to agree to take me on the cruise.'

'Kind?' He raised his brows. 'Did I have any option but to agree to take you on the cruise?'

Both George and Floria looked sharply at him. Their action set Judy thinking, for it clearly betrayed astonishment that Chris should make such an admission as that.

'Surely you're not saying Judy bullied you into taking her?' George spoke at last, his words accompanied by a half laugh of disbelief.

Chris answered without much expression,

'That, George, is exactly what I am saying.'

Floria actually gasped, then treated her sister-in-law to a look of profound admiration. For her part, Judy remained thoughtful, one half of her jubilant at her success, while the other half warned her that all was not as it appeared on the surface. She looked at Chris; he was intent on the music, tapping his fingers rhythmically on the table, apparently oblivious of anything but the melody, which was a waltz, romantic and slow. Suddenly aware of her gaze fixed upon him, he turned his head; a smile hovered on his lips for a space before he lost interest in her again.

'Well,' said George on recovering from the shock his friend's words had given him, 'I must congratulate you, Judy. Chris is the last man from whom I'd have expected an admission like that. Aren't you proud of yourself?'

Judy glanced uncertainly at Chris. He appeared not to have heard George's comments, because he was now humming the tune to himself.

'Yes,' she answered, but rather hesitantly, one eye still on her husband. 'I s-suppose I am proud of—of myself.' But she frowned in thought. She had certainly not bullied her husband—but she had been a trifle peevish and defiant, she recollected, insisting her tears were shed solely because she wanted so desperately to go on the cruise. But then Chris had expressed his disbelief, not in so many words, it was true, but his doubts were evident for all that. Still, in the end he had told her quite frankly that they were going on the cruise simply because he was letting her have her own way.

And suddenly Judy was swelling with triumph—quite forgetting that other half of her that had only moments ago warned that all was not as it appeared on the surface.

A short while later they left the café and sauntered along the arcades where the shops displayed fascinating glassware from Murano and beautiful lace from Burano and of course the lovely knitwear that always seemed to surpass any other in design, if not always in quality.

The romance of the famous city was impossible to ignore and as they strolled along the sides of the square Judy experienced a sense of nearness to her husband and it seemed quite natural that he should slip an arm round her shoulders and keep it there. Window-gazing, they stopped now and then to stare, and Judy would twist round, in her enthusiasm drawing Chris's attention to something, and she would find herself close against him, with her fair head touching his shoulder. Once, he kissed the hairline on her temple and she blushed rosily and her lips quivered in an adorable smile as she looked up into his dark face.

Meanwhile, George and Floria had wandered on ahead, alone for a few precious moments, avidly grasping what fate so grudgingly doled out, and storing these treasures in the place lovers keep for such things. Judy watched them, walking with a space between them while yearning to be close.

The next day they all left the hotel together to explore the city and it was natural that they should begin with St. Mark's, the fantastically beautiful church with its different styles of architecture and its fabulous treasures, many of which were taken as loot from Constantinople, while its marbles and golden mosaics often dated from as far back as the thirteenth century.

The exploration of the church took two hours, but

they could have stayed all day and not seen everything as they would have liked to see it. When they came out into the brilliant sunshine again Floria said she wanted to see the Doge's Palace, and then it was that the idea suddenly came to Judy. George had mentioned that Chris had been to Venice many times, so it was reasonable to assume he had been into the Doge's Palace.

'I feel like being outside,' she said, smiling at them in turn before her eyes settled on Chris's face. 'Do you mind very much if we don't go? Floria and George can go, of course,' she added, hoping she sounded as casual as she intended to do.

Floria looked at the ground; George did not bat an eyelid as he said,

'Are you sure, Judy? Aren't you keen to go into the Palace?'

She shook her head.

'We've been in the church all this time and I would prefer to be outside for a while. Do you mind?' she inquired again of her husband.

'As a matter of fact I also prefer to be outside, but——' He glanced apologetically at George. 'It's not very sociable of us to leave you and Floria——'

'Nonsense. We'll wander round on our own and then meet you somewhere for lunch—if that's all right with you?' His ready smile appeared; Judy smiled in response and assured him the arrangements suited her admirably, but glanced again at Chris. He nodded and they went their separate ways, George and Floria to the Palace and Judy and Chris to wander at random down the back streets, along some of the smaller canals, before finding themselves once more in the vicinity of the Piazza San Marco. They stood on a bridge and looked along the canal to the famous Bridge of Sighs; they were two among hundreds of holidaymakers and yet

Judy experienced again that sense of detachment from the world, of being alone with her husband. It was a magical, exciting sensation; she was gripped by a force she could neither understand nor control, yet a moment later she was floating through some heady atmosphere where, touched by the gentle breath of dawn, she stirred ... and awoke. Bewildered and unsure of herself, she turned, looking up at Chris as if she were seeing him for the first time. He smiled at her, but then, noting her expression, his smile faded and he looked questioningly at her.

'Little one, what is it?' She just shook her head, continuing to stare at him. A soft laugh broke from his lips. 'If you look at me like that another second, I shall be forced to kiss you.'

Colour rushed to her cheeks as she glanced away, down the canal again to the famous bridge. On the canal, boats were passing to and fro, carrying goods, not people.

'I'd like to—to sail in a gondola,' she stammered. 'On the—on the Grand Canal.'

He frowned at her, half in perplexity, half in amusement.

'Whatever you wish,' he returned obligingly, but went on to add, 'We'll have to leave it until after lunch, though, because we haven't time now. We're meeting Floria and George in just over half an hour.'

'Yes, of course we are. Can we go later, then?'

He nodded.

'We can all go together.'

'I expect you've been before—many times?'

'Not many times. Once in a gondola is usually enough.' They were standing very close, hemmed in by people. 'It's a novelty; once you've done it you're satisfied.'

'Perhaps you'd be bored, then?'

'Not at all. Besides, I'm here to oblige you, my dear.'

Her eyes gleamed suspiciously, but Chris was smiling at her and the idea that his voice was tinged with amusement was swiftly dispelled.

'Shall we go?' she suggested after a while. 'It's becoming rather a crush here.' She still knew the stirrings of an emotion that had hitherto lain dormant; she quivered as Chris took her arm and tucked it into his. They strolled on to the Rialto Bridge and Chris had to draw her attention to the glittering shops along the roadway, for she was in a world outside such mundane things.

They stopped under a central high arch and gazed along the world's most splendid highway, the Grand Canal, to the Palladian palaces and Gothic mansions, one-time homes of wealthy merchants but now used for other purposes like municipal offices and art galleries.

The bridge led to the Rialto markets. Chris stopped at a fruit stall and bought some enormous peaches.

'For you to eat on the gondola,' he laughed, swing the bag in one hand and taking Judy's arm with the other.

Floria and George were awaiting them when they arrived at the appointed meeting place and after finding a suitable restaurant they went in and had lunch. Several times during the meal Judy cast Floria a glance from under her lashes, but nothing was to be read in the Greek girl's face. George was his customary jovial self and Judy could not help admiring them both for their excellent acting.

Chris told them of Judy's suggestion that they hire a gondola and take a trip along the Grand Canal; the others were quite agreeable, and after leaving the gondola station near the Piazza San Marco they were soon travelling along an incredible waterway strewn on both sides with some of the most magnificent Renaissance architecture in the world. Palace after palace glided away behind them as even more magnificent residences took their place.

Judy brought her eyes from the splendour around her as she felt her husband's amused gaze fixed upon her.

'I'm so confused,' she laughed. 'I don't know which side to look.'

'That's how I am,' Floria put in. 'I'm so afraid of missing something.'

'You're bound to miss something,' said George. 'One could travel along here a hundred times and still miss something.'

They had passed under the Rialto Bridge by this time. The Canal pulsated with life; gondolas glided by carrying their wide-eyed tourists and rather bored gondoliers; *vaporetti* and *motoscafi* chugged along at a less leisurely pace, stopping at every station to allow their passengers to surge out, jamming one another with total disregard for etiquette, and with a haste that could be likened to a crowd fleeing from a burning building.

'What about that for magnificence?' exclaimed George all at once. 'The builders of these palaces must have been millionaires!'

They were passing the Ca' d'Oro, or House of Gold, a perfect example of the way in which the wealthy merchants of Venice displayed their opulent and extravagant tastes. Originally, gold decorations had been lavishly splashed all over the peerless façade. Colour was also used unsparingly, but although the building was Gothic in character it possessed a sumptuousness which seemed to brand it oriental.

Both girls gasped in wonderment as the architectural pageant unfolded before them. There was the more simple Renaissance Palazzo Fontana, and the Palazzo Corner del Regina; there was the magnificent Palazzo Pesara and the elaborate white baroque façade of the Church of San Stae.

'It wasn't long enough,' sighed Floria as the trip came to an end. 'I wish I could come here for a holiday.' A swift glance at George and then a lowering of her eyes. Not difficult to read her thoughts, Judy decided. Venice would be a wonderful place to come to with George. . . .

A sigh escaped Judy and she wondered again what Floria's father was like. No one had yet mentioned him; he appeared to be an outcast whom not one of his family had the least desire to see. He had made Floria marry Vincent, though, so he still maintained certain rights and authority.

'You might come for a holiday some time in the future,' George was saying in a rather gentle tone. Chris looked at him and said,

'It's most unlikely; Vincent isn't the man to take his wife travelling.'

Floria's lashes came down and something made Judy say,

'Chris and I might come one day, and then you can come with us, Floria.'

Judy received a mild stare from her husband, who made no comment on what she had just said.

'Have we time for some tea?' George wanted to know, breaking into the tense little silence that had for some reason descended on them all.

Chris glanced at his watch and nodded. They made their way to a café in one of the arcades in the Piazza where they had afternoon tea and listened to the lilting strains of the orchestra. People were milling about in their hundreds; it was a fantastic scene of colour and splendour and gaiety enacted under the dazzling blue of a cloudless Venetian sky.

And then it was time for them to return to the hotel to collect the luggage. Floria and George were going aboard with Judy and Chris, but on reaching the quay they all stood looking up at the graceful *Andromeda*, all white and gleaming and festooned with bunting because it was her maiden voyage.

'Oh,' breathed Floria, tilting her head right back, 'I wish I were coming with you!' So wistful her voice, and tinged with longing and envy. A slight frown gathered between her brother's eyes and noticing this Judy gave a sudden intake of her breath. Hitherto Chris had never revealed any interest in Floria and Judy had somehow gained the impression that he had little or no affection for her. This had seemed strange, because in Cyprus men were devoted to their sisters, protecting them and always showing concern for their happiness. Judy continued to stare at Chris, and she saw his mouth tighten as if he were angry about some-thing all at once.

'So do I wish I were coming with you,' George was saying enviously, but he added, 'I'll make an effort next year to take a trip on her, probably at Easter.'

Floria looked at him and then she lowered her head. If he took the trip it would have to be on his own, they were both thinking, and a terrible bleakness had ent-ered Floria's eyes when a moment later she looked up as Chris suggested they go on board.

'Can I see your cabin?' asked Floria, throwing off her unhappiness as she eagerly asked the question. Judy's expression became veiled; Chris threw her a smile of sardonic amusement before he turned to Floria and shook his head.

'You three stay on deck here while I see the luggage is safely taken away. I'll be with you in a few minutes.'

There was time to explore the ship and on Chris's

return they wandered around. George and Floria uttered more envious exclamations as they entered the ballroom and then the restaurant. There were the two night clubs, the sun decks and sports deck and the swimming pools. Eventually they found a quiet place to sit on the top deck, away from the bustling crowds and the noise. Judy, looking at Chris, wondered a little apprehensively if he would be bored with the trip. He preferred peace and quietness, she knew, and that was why he had a house on Hydra, high in the hills, and a house in the mountain village of Karmi in Cyprus. He would not have much peace and quietness on a trip of this nature, she thought, wondering if she had made a mistake in forcing him to take her on the cruise.

The voice of one of the hostesses over the air informed them that it was time for the visitors to leave the ship, and after kissing her brother and sister-in-law Floria followed George down the gangway and on to the quay where they stood until the ship moved slowly away. Judy and Chris stood by the rail, Judy waving all the time while Chris merely gazed down, appearing to be bored. Several times Judy stole a glance at him, and when at last George and Floria turned and walked away that tiny frown appeared between his eyes again. But that was all, Judy noticed with some considerable relief. Chris was concerned about Floria's not being too happy with her husband, but he had not the slightest inkling that she and George were in love.

Chris glanced down at Judy and said,

'Well, do you want to see your cabin?'

'Yes, please,' she replied demurely, and he laughed.

He allowed her to have her pick, but she would not at first agree to that.

'You should have the first choice,' she told him, looking round the second cabin to which he had taken her. 'Do you want this one? It has a verandah.'

'The choice is yours, my dear. Haven't I said I'm here to oblige you?'

She blinked at him uncertainly and said,

'I think it's only fair for you to have the best cabin, Chris. This one has the verandah, but the other's larger....' She tailed off because of the amusement in his eyes. He seemed always to be laughing at some secret of his own, she thought, subjecting him to a little frown of censure.

'Don't fuss, little one,' he begged. 'Is this the one you prefer?'

She nodded then, and as all the luggage had been put in the other cabin Chris went and brought hers along for her.

'Dinner's at half past eight,' he told her on turning to go.

'Half past eight? Won't I see you before then?'

'I've some writing to do. Have a walk round the ship for an hour, and then it'll be time to get yourself changed.'

Judy stared at the closed door; it seemed an eternity till half past eight....

A week later they were in Alexandria, having called at several Greek islands on the way, and also at Piræus, from where they went by taxi to Athens and spent a few hours in Judy's favourite place—the Acropolis. They then bathed in the sea at Cape Sounion, returning to the ship in time for dinner, and sailing away from Piræus later in the evening.

The ship was to remain in Alexandria for two days; passengers could either stay in that city, returning to the ship for meals and for sleeping, or they could go to Cairo by coach or taxi and from there they would be taken to the Pyramids.

'I don't think we'll join in with the organized trip.'

Chris had decided earlier, and Judy knew that by this time he was becoming tired of the crowds and the noisy activity that went on until the early hours of the morning. Also, it had leaked out that Chris was a member of the company owning the shipping line and for a couple of days or so everyone on the *Andromeda* seemed intent on meeting him and shaking hands with him. That he was annoyed was evident, although he managed to display a courteous enough front to his 'customers'. Judy, however, received the brunt of his annoyance and on one occasion he was so sharp with her that she almost wished she had not asserted herself and made him come on the trip.

'You mean we'll go by ourselves, by taxi?' she asked, recalling that the Naughtons, the middle-aged couple sharing their table in the restaurant, were also loath to go on the organized trip to Cairo. They had been looking round for someone to share a taxi in order to cut the cost of the fare, it being over a hundred and thirty miles from Alexandria to Cairo.

'Yes,' replied Chris. 'I couldn't face a coachload of chattering women and squealing children.'

She had to smile. The men, it would appear, would do nothing to aggravate him!

'Shall we share a taxi with the Naughtons, then?'

'No, my dear, we shall not.' Firm and deliberate was his decision. Judy would have liked the company of the Naughtons, but she did not think she would insist. No, on this occasion she would allow him his own way because she rather thought any argument on her part would lead to unpleasantness between them. This she would deeply have regretted because she meant her first visit to this most fascinating and mysterious city of the East to be a happy and memorable occasion. Often in the past she had dreamed about it, mentally sailing down the Nile in a *felucca*, standing in awed silence

117

before the treasures of Tutankhamen in the museum in Liberation Square, entering barefoot into the great mosque of Ahmed Ibn Tulun. She had visualized eating *kebabs* in a houseboat café on the banks of the sacred river, of watching the sun go down behind the Pyramids and seeing it rise again at dawn. She had wandered through the streets of Cairo buying flowers and souvenirs; she had gazed up into the sky to look into the face of a Nubian—for she had been told by her grandfather that the Nubians were *enormous*!

When the time came for them to leave the ship and step on to Egyptian soil Judy was so excited that she trembled visibly. Chris noted this and a faint smile touched the corners of his mouth; he made no comment, however, and within less than ten minutes they were in a taxi, the road taking them through the Nile Delta where thick marshy vegetation covered the swamps and where men kept appearing, up to their waists in water, fishing for something.

'What are they trying to catch?' she asked Chris, who was also interested in the men.

'I don't know—— Look, that one's caught something. It's wriggling, can you see? It looks like an eel.'

Judy looked, and swallowed. The thing was wriggling, as Chris said, and it seemed from this distance to be covered in mud and slime.

'Do they eat them?' she asked, feeling quite sick.

'I don't expect they go to all this trouble just for amusement,' he returned with a touch of humour.

The desert was more to Judy's liking, although it soon became monotonous as mile after mile was covered and there was at times absolutely nothing to see. Then there would appear a camel train on the horizon or a few stunted trees growing, no higher than bushes and warped by the wind. Sometimes they would pass a hovel made of sacks fastened to sticks plunged into the sand; sometimes they would see an Arab family—parents and several ragged children—far away from anywhere.

'There isn't any water!' exclaimed Judy. 'Why are they there, wandering about when there isn't even water to drink? And what do they live on? How can the goats find food when there's nothing but sand?'

Chris laughed at her expression, asking which question she would like answered first.

'I don't understand why they're here.' She threw out her hands, indicating the solitary road running through miles and miles of desert with absolutely nothing to see except this family, wandering along a few yards from the road, the woman carrying a baby on her back and the man walking beside three other children, and his two goats bending their heads to the barren ground. 'Where are they *going*?'

Again he laughed.

'Shall I stop the taxi and get out and ask them?' he inquired, and Judy blushed. Nevertheless, she said insistently,

'There isn't anything, anywhere—so where can they be going?'

'They're nomads. They just wander about.'

She allowed the matter to drop, feeling rather foolish, but she still wondered how these people lived—existed was a more fitting word, she thought, twisting her head to take a last look at the bedraggled family whose two goats of skin and bone appeared to be the total sum of their worldly goods.

The sun was beating down and a shimmering heat haze spread like elusive tulle across the parched and barren land. Nomads appeared again, this time on the other side of the road. The man carried a filthy bag on his back, the woman trudged along, like the other, a brown-faced baby on her back. The man stopped to watch the taxi; his lips parted to reveal a few stumpy black teeth as he grinned at the occupants. Judy waved and the man raised his hand. The tears pricked Judy's eyes. What was wrong in the world that human beings had to live like this—without homes, without proper food and clothing, tortured by the merciless sun during the day and by the intense cold at night? She suddenly felt ashamed that she had all the comforts money could buy, but her one deep emotion was pity, pity she could not control, and the tears streamed down her face.

'Judy ... little one!' Chris had turned his head and as he saw her tears he uttered the exclamation. 'What's wrong?'

She shook her head and wept all the more—and then she was in her husband's arms, her head against his breast, ashamed of her emotions and yet unable to stem her tears.

'It's so—so awful! Why don't people do something for them?'

'Hush, you silly child. They're used to this life; they were born to it. They don't know anything else.'

'What has that to do with it? Why isn't something being done!'

'Something is being done,' he assured her patiently. 'Wait until we reach the irrigated part, then you'll see a difference. These nomads wouldn't thank you for putting them into houses and making them go out to work every morning.' He drew a clean white handkerchief from his pocket and, gingerly taking the soaked little scrap from her fingers, he dried her eyes. 'Come now, I shall begin to wish I hadn't brought you if you go on like this. You're on holiday, child. You've come here to enjoy yourself.'

'I feel so guilty.'

He had to laugh, even though he knew he would

receive a plaintive and censorious glance from his wife.

'You're a very silly child to feel guilty. Have you contributed to any—er—discomfort these people may be suffering?'

'No, but neither have I contributed to any cause which might relieve their suffering.'

He gave an amused but faintly exasperated little sigh and took his arm from around her. She leant back against the upholstery and gazed out of the window. A few flatroofed houses now and some other buildings. Electric wires overhead ... she had always considered them ugly, wondering why they could not be taken underground, but now their appearance brought her an odd, ridiculous sort of comfort.

More miles of desert, flat and monotonous, and then trees! Here was where irrigation had begun, Chris told her. The desert was becoming productive, but these things took time. He spoke softly and soothingly, and she became calm; the dry sobs which were the aftermath of her tears ceased abruptly and she turned to give Chris a sheepish smile as she said,

'I'm silly, aren't I?'

'Yes, dear, you are.' But there was no amusement now in his attitude towards her, and no impatience. In fact, there was a new tenderness about him which moved her profoundly, stirring her memory to bring a fleeting recurrence of that magical, heady sensation she had experienced when standing beside her husband on the bridge in Venice. What was this feeling? She could have believed it to be the beginnings of love had her heart not already been given to Ronnie. Ronnie.... She had not thought of him for a long while ... but hadn't she made a determined effort to be brave and put him out of her mind? Her musings were checked by Chris's drawing her attention to the camel train on the skyline, far away across the wide desert.

'Three young ones; can you see them?' The quivering haze hung over the sand, but Judy could make out the young camels quite clearly.

'Yes; oh, I wish they were nearer! They look so sweet, and sort of helpless, walking so slowly beside their mothers.' She then added unconsciously, 'Will there be any water over there for them?'

'Not again, Judy, please. Camels can manage without water for ages. You know that.'

'The big ones, yes, but what about the little ones?'

'Apparently they manage to survive, otherwise the species would die out.'

She nodded absently, still watching the camels. There was something unreal about the silhouettes across the sand. The scene ought to be on a Christmas card, she thought.

'Are we nearly there?' she asked after a while. The vegetation was becoming more lush and healthy-looking. There were buildings all the time now, and vehicles.

'There are still a few miles to go; you'll see the buildings thickening up very soon now.'

At last they were in the city, an oasis in the wilderness—Cairo, largest of all desert cities. Excitement caught Judy again; she forgot everything but the thrill of reaching the city she had longed to enter since the time when she became old enough to read about it.

She also knew where she wanted to stay, and she spoke before Chris could mention Shepheard's or the Hilton.

'Can we stay at the Semiramis?'

'Do you know it?' he asked, puzzled.

'I've read about it. It's massive, and was once very splendid—when the English used to have lots of servants with them and needed many rooms. Can we stay there?'

'You're an old-fashioned little puss, aren't you? Are you sure you don't want the Hilton?'

She shook her head vigorously.

'No, it's the Semiramis I want.'

'Then the Semiramis it is.' Leaning forward, he gave instructions to the driver and soon they were there, at the hotel overlooking the Nile, with Shepheard's to one side of them and the Hilton a short distance away on the other.

'Oh!' she breathed on entering her room. 'I knew it would be like this!' The room was indeed massive. She moved swiftly to the window and stepped out on to the balcony. It looked west over the water. She turned into the room again, aware that Chris was standing there, regarding her quizzically. The Arab porter stood by him, holding his suitcase, but Judy continued to explore. The bathroom was also massive, and splendid. There was a dressing-room and inside this was the largest wardrobe Judy had ever seen. 'They must have had hundreds of dresses!' she exclaimed on emerging from the dressing-room.

'Or suits,' commented Chris and, turning, he went off with the porter to his own room next door.

But after a very quick wash and brush-up Judy went out on to the landing, intending to go to Chris. An unsmiling Arab appeared as if by magic and she stepped back into her room and pushed the door to. After waiting a few moments she went out again. The same Arab appeared—out of thin air, it seemed to Judy. Again she stepped back, frowning. A few more minutes passed and then, cautiously and soundlessly, she pulled the door inwards. Peeping out, she saw the great wide landing was empty and on tiptoe she made for Chris's door. The Arab appeared and she gave one final leap, almost crashing against the door.

'What on earth——?' Chris turned from the mirror,

a comb in his hand. Judy, rather breathless, and very white, was by the door, her hands behind her back, pushing against it as if she anticipated imminent invasion. 'You look as if you've seen a ghost. What's wrong?'

Fear had lodged in her throat and she swallowed hard to remove it.

'That man——' Vaguely she pointed over her shoulder. 'He kept coming out every time I came from my room. Wh-what d-does he want?'

A broad grin replaced the frown on Chris's face. But he did not answer her question immediately.

'Every time you came from your room? What were you leaving your room for?'

'I was coming to you—because I was ready and didn't want to waste any time.'

'Away from me, you mean?' was his swift inquiry, accompanied by a flicker of amusement in his eye.

She flushed.

'I want to start seeing things right away,' she said, and his face fell with mock disappointment.

'The man out there merely wanted a tip,' he then informed her.

'A tip?' She blinked at him. 'What for?'

The grin reappeared on Chris's face.

'Not for anything in particular. These men dart out from some mysterious hiding-place and, for some reason I can never understand, expect you to give them a tip.'

'For doing nothing?'

'They ring for the lift for you or, in the case of the ladies, offer to carry their handbags downstairs for them.' He looked at her with an odd expression as she came farther into the room. 'What did you think he wanted?' The shrewd inflection in his tone caused an increase in her colour again.

'I couldn't make out what he wanted,' she replied evasively.

He made no comment on that, although his brow lifted sceptically. But there was only amusement in his voice as he said, turning to the mirror again and applying the comb to his hair,

'If you decide you require male protection during the night just thump on the wall. I'll rather enjoy rescuing a damsel in distress.' His eyes met hers through the mirror; she noticed the sudden light of mockery in them and lowered her head. Yet she was dwelling on the careless way in which he spoke those words—with no sign of anger or a darkling look—and she thought again how westernized he was, and enlightened. On her marriage she had taken it for granted he would be no different from the average Greek or Cypriot husband: he would treat her as a possession and, therefore, regard every other man who came near her in the light of a trespasser. But Chris was not like that at all; the first time she had noticed this difference was when he made her wear those brief shorts. It was as if he didn't mind at all if other men looked at her so long as she was attractive for *him*. Perhaps, mused Judy as she glanced up again and saw him making the final draw of the comb through his hair, she should not have adopted that determined attitude of man-management, for she had a shrewd suspicion that had she taken the trouble to investigate his character she would soon have made the discovery that he did not require 'managing' at all.

CHAPTER SEVEN

CHRIS insisted on their having lunch in the hotel before going off on their sightseeing expedition. Judy had no time for food and she told him so.

'We'll eat, nevertheless,' he said firmly, and they went into the restaurant. On their way out again Judy stopped in the foyer and stared at the massive figure of the commissionaire standing there.

'He must be at least seven feet tall,' she whispered to her husband.

'Every inch of seven feet.' Chris, at well over six feet, had also to look up at the handsome Nubian. The man smiled at Judy and she thought she had never seen a more attractive man—other than Chris, of course, who for some unfathomable reason was in Judy's eyes becoming more attractive every day. 'Your manners, child!' Whispered words, but admonishing; she gave the man another smile and followed her husband who was already making for the street.

The Nile, sacred river of the Egyptians through aeons of time, shimmered in the sun which blazed down on the bustling city. The water was blue-green and docile; even when it swelled in late summer it could be subdued—not like that other great Arab river, the Greek name for which was Tiger. The Tigris of Iraq was a violently rapacious river, flooding inconveniently in the spring when water was not required. But the gentle Nile had always flooded in the summer, bringing life to the thirsty land. Nowadays the waters were controlled by dams, and at the Barrage above Cairo they were held back against the thirsty months of drought. And the Nile was also an accommodating waterway, its northward-flowing movement taking boats to the Mediterranean, while the prevailing wind coming from that sea assisted the boats on their return journey.

'Can we go on a *felucca*?' asked Judy excitedly as they crossed the road and stood looking at the river. A tawny-skinned boatman was waiting expectantly for more customers to fill his partly-laden vessel. The next moment Judy was walking gingerly across a rickety plank, Chris's firm hand under her arm. They sat together in the boat; the sails flapped as the *felucca* skimmed the water, heading for Al-Gamia, the University Bridge.

Their sail lasted an hour; Judy was flushed and excited, avidly taking in the scene of bustling activity along the bank, the lovely buildings and mosques and minarets, the palm trees on the water's edge and the lovely bougainvillea with their floral bracts of glowing red or purple. Dusky figures moved like extras on a crowded stage, some in white flowing cotton robes and others in stripes, their feet shod in leather slippers and on their heads white caps or turbans. It was an oriental scene, alive and vital, yet mysterious and bewildering.

In bygone days when the August floods were expected from the interior of Africa the whole of Cairo would turn out to celebrate the event of *wafaa al-Nil*—the faithfulness of the Nile. The Nile, however, was on occasions a little dilatory and then the long procession would be entreating, not thanking. The Sultan in his jewelled robes would lead the priests of Islam in a united evocation to the Nile to be generous. In very ancient times an added incentive would be the pagan rite of casting alive into the river a beautiful maiden—'the bride of the Nile'—as a sacrifice. In the days of the Pharaohs the life-giving flood waters of this mighty river were believed to be the tears of Isis, goddess of the earth's fruits, mourning for Osiris. In more recent times the Nile, like the Bosphorus, was a dungeon of abandoned hope into which wrongdoers would be thrown, trussed and still breathing.

'Did you enjoy it?' Chris asked the question as they left the boat and began strolling along the waterfront again.

'It was marvellous!' She looked up at him and added impulsively, 'Thank you for bringing me, Chris. I'm sure I'd never have come to Egypt if I hadn't been married to you. . . .' Her voice trailed away and a hint of colour touched the lovely contours of her face as her husband's brows rose a fraction.

'So marriage does have some compensations,' he commented drily, apparently determined to see that she was even more put out than at present.

'I don't think my grandfather would ever have brought me here,' she admitted willingly after an evasive hesitancy which she was unable to maintain owing to the persistent glances cast at her by Chris. 'Being married makes me . . . freer than I was before.'

'You feel freer with me than you did with your grandfather?' he asked curiously.

'In one way,' she owned. 'As I've just said, I'd never have seen Egypt had I not been married to you.'

'Tell me,' he said glancing down at her, 'are you glad or sorry that you consented to marry me?'

'Consented?' Judy left his question unanswered for a moment as she politely reminded him that she did not consent; she had not been consulted. Both he and her grandfather had forgotten she was British. She had been treated as a Cypriot girl obliged to obey her guardian, accepting the man he chose for her and not offering one word of protest. 'I was only fifteen, too,' she went on to add. 'That was very young for me to be forced into an engagement.'

A cold little silence followed, and as they walked along, making for nowhere in particular, Judy began to regret her outspokenness. She had never complained before—and indeed she wasn't really meaning to complain now—but had resignedly settled down to the life which fate had mapped out for her. Now, it seemed, she had vexed him and a coolness was surely going to mar their holiday ... unless she could repair the damage she had quite inadvertently done to the rather pleasant relationship which had begun to develop between them.

'I understand, then, that you're telling me you wouldn't have been forced into the engagement had you been older?' Judy did not answer because an answer was too difficult. All her thoughts were contradictory these days. Sometimes she would reflect on what marriage to Ronnie would have been like, but the picture seemed to have entirely lost its charm, for she was daily growing closer to Chris, experiencing pleasant sensations when they drifted into moments of intimacy like those on the bridge in Venice—and those when Chris took it into his head to kiss her. She told herself one minute that he had married her for desire, while in the next bewildering moment she would wonder why, if his desire had been so strong, he was able to resist coming to her. True, she had laid down the law to him regarding that, but her idea that he was docile and meek had already undergone some modification even before she witnessed George's astonished disbelief when Chris baldly admitted that he'd been bullied by his wife into taking her on the cruise. Floria too had been amazed by her brother's admission, so it was reasonable to assume Chris had always been regarded by Floria as a strong-willed man whose wife would be kept well and truly under his domination. In addition, Judy had herself owned more than once that her husband could master her if he chose, although it was true that each time she acknowledged this she found herself back to the argument Lefki had made: men were basically all the same, 'stand up to them and they'll usually see eye to eye because it's less wearing than being forever in a tussle with you'.

Judy drew a deep breath, wishing she could sort out this untidy muddle of her thoughts. There was the gnawing little suspicion that Chris was often deriving some sort of amusement from their relationship, that he was enjoying himself at her expense; there was also the question of Corinne, who had been much more than a friend and who was still in love with Chris. Judy was sure Chris was not in love with Corinne, but she felt equally sure he was human enough to continue accepting any favours that Corinne proved willing to give. 'I've asked you a question, Judy.' Her husband's soft voice put an end to her musings and she was again filled with a desire to repair the damage she had done by her unnecessary reference to the injustice she had suffered in being forced into her engagement to Chris. But she had to be truthful, and this meant frankly admitting that had she been older she would most certainly have put forward some sort of protest. But after that she added, in answer to his first question,

'Nevertheless, I cannot truthfully say now that I'm sorry I married you, Chris.' The simple confession, softly and sincerely spoken, was more eloquent than anything else she could have said, and it was also more touching. Chris slipped an arm about her shoulders, then his hand found her waist and stayed there, caressingly.

'Fifteen was young, my dear,' he said gently. 'As you've remarked, it was very young for you to be forced into an engagement.'

His words naturally surprised her and she glanced up swiftly. He was staring at the road ahead and she was unable to read his expression. But there was an air of sadness about him, she thought—or could it be regret? At the idea that it might be regret dismay out of all proportion flooded over her and she faltered, automatically placing her hand over the back of his as it gently gripped her waist.

'Can I ask you the same question you asked me?' and when he looked inquiringly at her, 'Are you glad—or—or sorry you married me?' Her sweet young face was pale; her lips quivered. These he noticed and a wondering light filled his eyes.

'I knew, the moment I saw you, that I wanted to marry you—and I haven't changed my mind, Judy. I'm not that sort of person.' Gravely he spoke, in English as always, his tones rich and deep. She was far from satisfied with the answer he had given her, although she could not have produced a reason for this.

'What made you offer for me—when I was so young, as you have just admitted?'

The hint of a smile, the almost imperceptible lift of a brow.... These seemed to give Judy her answer even before he spoke..

'I was afraid that if I left you to grow up I'd be too late—that someone else would offer for you.'

Her heart sank and a long trembling sigh left her lips. She had always known why he offered for her, had been fully aware desire was all that had been in his mind. And only seconds ago this stark truth had been revealed in those two small but meaningful gestures. So why should her heart sink at his words? For what other answer had she yearned?

Judy knew, without any doubts at all, what answer she had desired. And yet how stupid she was. Had she, in all the years she had lived in Cyprus, known of any man who had offered because he loved the girl? A man saw, then desired, then assessed, and finally he went into the matter of a dowry. How much had her grandfather given Chris? she wondered. The matter had been so humiliating, because she was British, that Judy had cast it away, and the question of a dowry had never once been mentioned between her grandfather and herself.

Her sudden revelation filled her whole being. She had never for one moment visualized falling in love with this dark Greek, this man whom she had at first regarded with no small sense of fear. She recalled his fury on hearing about her meetings with Ronnie. How possessive he had been! And how he had frightened her. Perhaps he would be like that again, she thought, should a similar occasion arise. But no similar occasion could arise—unless she saw Ronnie again, which was most unlikely.

'Little one,' said Chris at last. 'What are you thinking?'

She awoke from her reverie and looked up. He was smiling in a way that set her heart racing and she determinedly put up a guard. But she would not be cool with him, because she was here in this wonderful city, where she had always wanted to be, and nothing was going to detract from the pleasure she had for so long anticipated. Besides, nothing had really changed; Chris did not love her, but she had known and accepted this. Affection could still enter her marriage, as she had intended it to when she suggested they 'keep company'.

'I was thinking of all sorts of things,' she frankly replied, returning his smile. 'But right now I am thinking about where I want to go next.'

'And where do you want to go next?'

'To the old city to buy some presents, and to the mosque of Ahmed Ibn Tulun, because everyone goes there. It will be time to go back to the hotel for dinner then, but——' She hesitated, then went on diffidently, 'Can we go to a night club?' She had heard of the belly-dancers and wanted to see them, for in Cyprus the girls did not dance in night clubs. This was done by foreign women—French and English and other nationalities.

Chris might have read her thoughts and, westernized as he was, he had no intention of relaxing to that extent. In Greece or Cyprus he would not have taken his wife to a night club of that kind, and he would not do so here.

'No, Judy, we can't.'

Silence. Should she insist? Lefki would have insisted. . . .

'But I want to go. I've never been to one——'

'And you're not likely ever to do so,' he cut in softly. 'We'll be taking quite a long while over dinner, and then, after a little stroll we'll be ready for bed. If we're going to have a full day's sightseeing tomorrow we'll have to be up early.' The two major items for the following day were the Pyramids and Sphinx at Giza, and the Pharaonic museum in Liberation Square.

'We needn't stay long,' began Judy when she stopped, warned by one quelling glance.

'Careful, Judy,' he advised, and added cryptically, 'Don't go too far or you'll spoil everything. You've told me of your plans for the rest of today and I'm quite willing to do what *you* want to do.' He paused a moment and withdrew his arm from around her. 'This evening we shall do what *I* want to do, and that won't be visiting a night club.'

Judy remained silent, her head lowered. This, she surmised, was the point beyond which it was imprudent to go.

She missed his arm, warm and gentle, on her back, and his hand on her waist. It was her own fault, but she felt miserable all the same. She inquired at length if they were anywhere near the mosque.

'We'll take a taxi,' was the rather abrupt reply, and after they had been in the taxi a few minutes she said meekly,

'I'm sorry, Chris.' She had not meant to be meek and apologetic, for that meant a retrograde step in her aim for equality, but her heart dragged abominably and she would have done anything to ease the tension that had dropped like a barrier between them. He shot a glance at her profile; her head was bent and she did not raise it. She was gazing fixedly at her hands, clasped on her lap. She looked the picture of misery and a relenting smile broke over her husband's dark and handsome face. He reached out and patted her hand. Her spirits rose. 'I didn't mean to be disagreeable.' She looked at his hand resting on hers and had an almost irresistible urge to raise it to her cheek.

'I know quite well you did not mean to be disagreeable,' he returned surprisingly. There was a dry edge to his tone, though, and she knew instinctively that he was fully aware that her intention had been to assert herself, aiming as always at having her own way.

Yes, she definitely decided, Chris knew what she was about—had done so from the first. Why, then, had he not resisted? His behaviour was incomprehensible and Judy thrust the matter from her, turning her thoughts to the pleasures in store.

The massive solemn square in which stood the ablution fountain of the Ibn Tulun Mosque was silent and awe-inspiring. It was an oasis of peace and serenity amid the turbulence and ugliness of crowded streets. The ugliness pressed right up to its gates, but once inside these gates there descended upon Judy an atmosphere that was outside time. Here her feet were on the soil of Islamic Cairo; nomads in ancient times had pitched their tents here—and here they had lived and died, free from the shackles of the modern civilization that was to come.

'Isn't it ... peaceful?' Judy whispered the words because that seemed the thing to do. Chris merely nodded, his concentrated gaze fixed on the oddly shaped, unconventional minaret.

'What happened there, I wonder?' he remarked at last. Used as he was to the elegant, slender minarets of the Turkish mosques in Cyprus, Chris regarded this contraption with acute dislike.

Judy looked up, and gave a little gasp.

'That's not a minaret?'

'Certainly it is, but it's more like a debased *ziggurat*. This Ibn Tulun must have been an eccentric.' At that moment a coach load of tourists filed through the gates and Chris and Judy exchanged glances of resignation.

'Never mind,' said Judy comfortingly. 'The guide will be useful.'

'We haven't paid,' began Chris, when he was interrupted.

'What does that matter? We'll shuffle along at the back and make ourselves small.'

'You make me feel quite old,' he said, taking her arm and proceeding towards the crowd gathered around the guide.

'Old? Why should I make you feel old?'

'Because you yourself are so young—and so uninhibited——' He broke off there and laughed. 'Uninhibited in *some* ways,' he qualified, and a swift rise of colour told him the malicious barb had found its mark.

'I said we must get to know one another better.' Her natural defensive instinct had been put into words before she could restrain it, and the rosy colour spread right up to her temples at the look her husband gave her.

'Darling,' he laughed, 'there is a time and place for the discussion of such things! Come, we're missing something.'

Darling.... It didn't mean a thing, of course. Men often called someone darling, as did women. No, it had no special significance—why should it?

The guide, round and dark-skinned and wearing a turban, was in a spotless white *galabiya* which, when Judy happened to get near him as they all entered the mosque, gave off the fresh clean smell of a garment newly laundered. She knew instinctively that whenever such a smell assailed her nostrils again she would think of Ali Baba. For that was what he asked the tourists to call him, although there were laughing protests that Ali Baba could not possibly be his name. With a grave countenance and unmoving eyes he assured them that it was, so everyone was left guessing. However, with the typical friendliness of guides all over the world Ali Baba had very soon created a happy carefree atmosphere and everyone joined in the laughter whenever he told a joke or related some humorous incident that had happened when he had been taking tourists around.

The oddly shaped minaret, he had already told them, came into existence because Ibn Tulun, noted for his impatience with idlers, was once seen amusing himself by folding a piece of paper into all sorts of odd shapes. Ashamed of being caught in this idle pastime, he made a swift recovery by saying that this was how he wished the minaret to look. The great mosque was at that time in the course of construction and the limestone minaret, looking very odd indeed because the base was square and the upper part circular, was duly erected in obedience to the great man's wishes. However, as the present minaret was dated much later than the ninth century—when the mosque was first built—the story could not very well be true.

The inside of the mosque was characterised by that coolness and air of spiritual and meditative restfulness which is found in any mosque, wherever it might be. Ali Baba sat down on one of the beautiful carpets covering the floor and his audience gathered around, entering into the spirit of this adventure in emulating his posture by squatting, cross-legged, on the carpet.

The history of the mosque was related, Ali Baba's audience learning how Ibn Tulun, coming to Egypt from a great city of Samarra, in Iraq, built a new city, with the magnificent mosque, a palace for himself and of course a hippodrome for polo, because all Turks and Arabs loved horses.

On emerging from the dim cool interior of the mosque everybody put on their shoes again and after the tourists had wandered around the courtyard taking snapshots, Ali Baba politely informed them that it was time to go. Chris had a few minutes previously managed to get him alone and offered to pay him, saying that he and his wife were not of the party, but Ali Baba would not hear of accepting money.

'You're staying at the Semiramis,' he said, as if this were sufficient reason why they should make use of his services.

'We are—but what has that to do with it?' Chris regarded Ali Baba in some puzzlement. 'And how did you know we're staying there?'

'I saw you arrive. I was waiting for these tourists; they'll be staying at the Semiramis.' He paused a moment. 'I don't know what plans you've made, of course, but I shall be escorting these same people to the Pyramids of Giza in the morning and you and your wife are very welcome—if you would care to join us, that is?'

'Yes,' intervened Judy, her voice bright and eager. 'Can we, Chris?'

Ali Baba's dark eyes rested on her face and before Chris could reply to her question he was speaking, softly, and with that timeless wisdom and insight known only to the people of the East.

'This combination of English and Greek ... what beauty it creates.' He transferred his gaze to Chris, having to look up even though he himself was by no means small. 'Your exquisitely fashioned wife *is* partly Greek, I think?'

'Her mother was a Greek Cypriot.' Chris smiled at his wife, searching her face.

'I knew. And you, sir? You are from Greece, not Cyprus.' A statement, and Chris nodded. 'You're a lucky man indeed.' He paused and then with the outspokenness that was also characteristic of the East he added twinklingly, his eyes roving over Judy's slender figure, 'It's easy to see why you chose her....' Chubby fingers were suddenly pressed to his mouth and then flicked away, while Ali Baba's eyes took on a dreamy, faraway expression. 'What pleasure she must give you! What ecstasy to be mated to such a divine creature!'

The blood rushed to Judy's cheeks and she dared not venture a glance at her husband. But she could picture the mocking amusement she would have encountered in his face; she could almost see the wry curve of his lips as he produced the smooth reply which would be expected from the eager man before them.

'How right you are, Ali Baba. The pleasure my wife gives me is indescribable.'

Judy did look up then—to glare at him. His eyes widened in a sort of warning gesture, but they held a kindling of humour as well, and suddenly both he and Judy burst out laughing.

'Now I wonder why you laugh?' murmured Ali Baba strangely. 'I wonder...' He fell silent a moment and then, 'Shall you be accompanying us in the morning?'

'Most certainly—and thank you very much for asking us.'

'You,' pronounced Judy with heat as the last of the tourists disappeared through the gate, 'were absolutely horrid!'

'A guilty conscience, eh? Serve you right!'

'Why do you let me have my own way?' she asked, quite out of the blue. He started but instantly recovered, obviously realizing she had spoken on impulse.

'I must bow to your will,' he replied woodenly, and Judy's lips pursed. 'What say do I have in the matter?'

I must bow to your will.... Judy's eyes narrowed. Those were almost the exact words she had written to Lefki.... 'Thank you for telling me what to do. It certainly works ... Chris bows to my will in most things....'

And Judy had left that letter around in her bedroom for days before putting it in an envelope and posting it....

'I shouldn't have imagined you to be so—so—er—co-operative.'

'Co-operative?' he laughed. 'That wasn't the word you intended to use.'

No, she had intended using the word 'meek', but some inner voice warned her this would be unwise.

'That first night,' she murmured, unable to comment on his latest remark, 'you didn't seem willing then to—to bow to my will, as you term it.'

'The first night?' He frowned in thought and she looked severely at him. He knew very well to what she referred and she felt tempted to inform him of her awareness that his questioning manner was feigned. However, she decided against it, unwilling to say anything which might bring about a recurrence of that coolness which had come between them only an hour or so ago.

'You were very sarcastic, asking me if you should bow yourself out—er—backwards.'

They were standing by the domed ablution fountain which was both functional as well as decorative, for here it was that those entering the mosque must first wash themselves. Visitors did not wash, of course, but men could often be seen using these ablution fountains. The sun blazed down and the air was humid and oppressive. Judy yawned behind a small brown hand and fleetingly there appeared an almost tender light in her husband's eyes. Yet his voice was crisp and faintly arrogant when at last he said,

'I expect it was shock at the decision you had reached. It isn't usual for a bridegroom to be shown the door on his wedding night.'

'I didn't show you the door!' she denied indignantly, quite oblivious of the fact that her words were irrelevant. They were also amusing, apparently, for a sudden gleam of laughter entered her husband's eyes. 'I would like to know, Chris, what is so funny?' She had meant to be coolly inquiring and faintly bored, stealing some of the dignity her husband often portrayed, but somehow her intention went awry. Chris threw back his head and laughed, at the same time taking both her hands in his and drawing her close to him.

'*You* are so funny!' He stopped laughing and gazed down into her face. 'Do you remember my saying it was going to be delightful being married to you?' She nodded vaguely, her eyes wide, her young lips softly parted, invitingly. 'Well, Judy, it *is*—quite soon, I think.' And on that rather obscure statement he slid his arms around her and kissed her gently on the lips. They were the sole occupants of the square. Silence

140

reigned; the peace and the calm entered into them both. Shyly Judy responded to her husband's kiss. 'Ali Baba was right in one thing,' he whispered close to her ear. 'You're beautiful ... and you're exquisitely fashioned.'

The vibrancy in his voice, the shadowed expression that could have been tenderness, the caress of his hands on her arms and the small pulsation of a vein in his neck ... Judy noted these things and bewilderedly endeavoured to translate them into a language she could understand, but this was impossible. Chris was holding her away from him, his handsome face serious, and very dark in the shadow cast by the domed building by which they stood. At last he shook his head, as if trying to clear it after partaking of some heady draught.

'Come, my dear,' he said matter-of-factly, 'we'll have to be getting a move on if you want to do this shopping you mentioned.'

The shops were fascinating to Judy. Typical of the East, they were literally bulging with merchandise. Displays, if they appeared at all, were muddled and unattractive. On the other hand, there was something exciting about having to look carefully and concentrate because there was such a vast array of goods to see..

'I want that.' Judy pointed to a silver medallion on a chain. It was in a glass case and Chris indicated to the white-robed assistant that he wished to see it. 'Do you like it?' Judy looked questioningly at her husband and after a careful examination of the object he nodded.

'Very pretty. Yes, we'll have that,' he told the assistant, who eagerly began wrapping it up in tissue paper. The medallion was beautifully worked by hand. Trees in filigree and animals in solid silver were surrounded by a fluted frame of silver, and a decorative loop attached it to the silver chain.

'How much was it?' Judy wanted to know as they moved on to the next counter.

'Mind your own business.'

Judy laughed and allowed the matter to drop. At the next counter they bought a bronze inlaid plaque of Nefertiti, and another of Tutankhamen and his queen.

'One of these is for Floria,' she explained when Chris pointed out the similarity of these two plaques, suggesting that she buy the one in wood carving which the smiling assistant was persistently thrusting before her eye. 'I like these better than the wooden ones.'

'What would you like me to buy you?' he asked when they were out in the street again, looking at other shops. There were masses of people about, many wearing the long cotton robes but many also wearing trousers and shirts. Stalls occupied the centre of the road and tourists were bargaining good-naturedly with their owners. The sun was still hot even though its rays were beginning to slant; the air was still sultry and perspiration could often be seen pouring down the faces of the tourists who were not used to the heat. Judy and Chris were used to such heat and it did not affect them as they strolled among the crowds, or stopped now and then to examine some object which caught Judy's eye.

'You've bought me the medallion,' she reminded Chris. 'That's all I want.' She had been searching for something for Chris, but had no idea what he would like.

'I heard you saying something to Floria about an Alexandrite ring.'

'Oh yes, I almost forgot! Lefki has one and it's beautiful. It changes colour—did you know that?'

He nodded.

'Alexandrite does change colour. Sometimes it's red and sometimes it's purple.'

'Yes, and all the shades in between,' she added. 'Do

you think we can buy one here?' She glanced round vaguely. 'I expect there were some in that first shop, but I suppose it's too far to go back?'

'It is, rather. We'll find some along here, though.'

It was almost seven o'clock when they returned to the hotel, Judy twisting the pretty ring on her finger and carrying a small ivory Buddha, exquisitely carved and very old. She had found it quite by accident in a small shop in a back street and had bought it for Chris. He had been so delighted with it that he pressed his lips to her temple, right there and then, and thanked her in a faintly husky voice.

'I'll keep it on my desk, where I can see it every day,' he promised gravely, and Judy felt a warmth spread through her because of the way he looked, and the way he smiled, as he said those words.

They had taken a taxi after finishing their shopping, and had travelled for miles round the back streets of Cairo. They had seen all kinds of houses, from the tenements of the *baladi* to the more spacious abodes of the middle-class, or *frangi*, as they were called. Their gardens boasted flowers which were familiar to both Chris and Judy—hibiscus and bougainvillea and poinsettia, and other exotic blooms whose perfume hung in the soft still air. They had visited another mosque, then stopped to watch the river traffic for a while. Then Judy had felt sorry for a street vendor because all the tourists were passing him by and patronizing another man a few yards away. Amused but resigned, Chris ordered the taxi driver to pull into the side of the road. Judy got out, and on returning a few minutes later she had two handfuls of trinkets—necklaces, brooches, earrings and bracelets.

'Only seventy piastres!' she exclaimed. 'How about that for a bargain?'

'Seventy? And you consider you've obtained a bargain?'

Dropping the trinkets into her lap, Judy then proceeded to examine them separately.

'Two scarab rings, four necklaces in silver——'

'In what!'

'Silver-coloured metal,' she conceded, looking at Chris in a half-amused, half-deprecating way. 'One ... two ... three—— Seven brooches with pretty stones——' She darted him a sideways glance, her eyes twinkling. 'Stones the colour of rubies. Then I have two pairs of earrings. Yes, of course I consider I've obtained a bargain!'

'It's all rubbish,' he returned mildly, taking up one of the brooches and frowning at it.

'Costume jewellery,' she insisted. But then she added, 'I can give it away when we get home. The little girls of the village will love these things.'

'What made you buy them, if you're only going to give them away?'

She blushed faintly, and spread her hands.

'The man had nothing else to sell.'

'So you just had to buy something?' With a totally unexpected movement he took her hand and gave it an affectionate squeeze. 'Yes, little one,' he murmured gently, almost tenderly, 'you're going to be delightful to live with.'

CHAPTER EIGHT

THE sun was up and the city bustling with life, but Judy lay in bed, stretched out luxuriously, and gave herself over to a pleasant reflective mood, there being plenty of time before she must take her bath and proceed downstairs to meet her husband at the breakfast table.

She had been awakened by the call to prayer from Cairo's minarets. This call to the faithful took place five times a day; men would leave what they were doing and proceed to the mosque of their preference and there they would pray, devout barefooted suppliants, their faces turned towards sacred Mecca, the city of Mohammed's birth, and to which all Cairo's mosques were orientated.

This summoning to prayer was no novelty to Judy, as it was to most tourists, because there were Muslims in Cyprus and, therefore, mosques in plenty. And from the minarets of these mosques the Turkish Cypriots would be called to prayer in exactly the same way as the Muslim inhabitants of Cairo, this desert city of Africa.

She dwelt on her activities of yesterday, and knew she was fortunate in being married to Chris. Her grandfather could have given her to someone else ... someone like Vincent, for example. Judy shivered. Vincent was oily and stout; he always seemed as if he required a shave and a shampoo. His clothes were never immaculate like those of Chris; his shirts were not changed even once a day. Chris on the other hand would change his several times if the weather were particularly hot. Judy changed several times too. This changing was necessary if one desired to keep fresh in a hot country.

Yes, her grandfather had really chosen well, Judy conceded as she lay there, gazing up at the high ceiling and the ornamental cornices portraying the splendour of this hotel in the days of the British administrators and businessmen. How different would have been her life had she been married to another Vincent, a man who would nauseate her and who would also imprison her. She would not have been allowed her own way with Vincent, or one of his kind, she felt sure. And her heart went out to Floria, and all the girls like her who were forced into marriages with men they could never respect, let alone love.

Yesterday.... Never had she packed so much into a few short hours. For after dinner they had walked for miles, although they had set out to take a short stroll along the waterfront. Chris had taken her hand immediately they left the hotel and had retained it for the whole of the time. He had kissed her cheek on one occasion and her head on another. Judy supposed it was the romance of this mysterious city, set in the desert yet with the life-giving aorta of the Nile running through it, making it unique in that it never knew thirst. There was a saying that 'who drinks the water of the Nile often can hardly bear to leave it'. If one did leave it, travelling a few miles east or west, one could die of thirst.

Judy yawned; she felt sleepy again, but she must not sleep. Today was the day for which she had waited almost all her life. Today she would see the Pyramids and the Sphinx!

A deep sigh of contentment left her lips. It seemed incredible that there ever was a time when she did not want to marry Chris ... and yet that time was less than two months ago!

At last she had to think of getting up. Her door was locked and she smiled to herself. The last thing Chris did was to remind her to bang on the wall if she required help. He had laughed with her when she had shown him the very adequate lock, with its large key ready to be turned the moment he left her. But his laugh had died away after a second or two and the most odd expression had settled on his face. Judy had experienced a certain degree of discomfort, brought on by an aggravating little devil of guilt that would not leave her alone. She had in the end felt she could have let her husband stay—but try as she would no suitable words, eloquent or otherwise, obligingly appeared to fill the gap in her vocabulary which she now saw as a chasm which was going to prove exceedingly difficult to bridge. It was hardly the thing to say, 'We know each other better now, so therefore you may stay.' In fact, she had the extraordinary conviction that should she say something of that nature her husband would don an armour of pride and tell her where to go!

Ali Baba was waiting when they came from breakfast into the entrance hall; gradually the other tourists assembled and then the coach arrived and they all made their way towards it.

From the heart of Cairo they drove along a broad modern highway with views of the open countryside beyond its edges. With the gradual thinning of the buildings the vista became one of low-lying fields and a few scattered houses, with occasionally a cluster of mud huts fringed by a circle of palms. And then, across the fields, there they were—the great mountains of stone, the Pyramids of Giza, built on a high desert plateau above Cairo.

'Oh,' breathed Judy, staring towards the great bulk of the Pyramid of Cheops. 'Chris, isn't that a magnificent scene!' The sun reflected back, leaving a tawny-gold translucence on the gigantic side of the Pyramid. 'What must they have been like when they were covered with alabaster, all glittering like mother-of-pearl? And can you imagine the Sphinx—her head hanging with priceless ornaments and her face painted a brilliant crimson?'

Chris merely smiled, for now a loud murmur ran through the coach as excitement began to mount and increase. The journey had taken less than half an hour, but the latter part had to be taken either by camel or pony and trap.

'Are we riding camels?' asked Judy as they left the bus. She looked up rather doubtfully at Chris, and was not at all surprised when he shook his head and declared emphatically,

'No camel for me, thank you, Judy. You can please yourself, of course.'

At that moment a driver brought his camel close. Precariously perched on its back was a giggling woman, urging the animal on in some way of her own, anxious to catch up with her friends who were leaving her behind. The smell of the camel was by no means pleasant and Judy decided that although she would have liked to boast of having ridden a camel she preferred to go with Chris in the trap.

Other tourists had arrived before them and there was a short wait for Chris and Judy until a trap was available. The place was rather crowded, and noisy. Cameras were snapping at laughing people standing beside camels or sitting on their backs. White-robed Arabs were hawking their wares—models of the Pyramids and Sphinx, leather goods and picture postcards and numerous other souvenirs which the tourists were eager to add to their collections.

At last the trap arrived and the couple it had brought down alighted. Judy and Chris took their places; at the pony's head a smiling Arab walked slowly, carrying a stick which he never used. Progress was slow, but there was no necessity for speed. Ali Baba was already there when they reached the Great Pyramid, talking to those of the party who had arrived at the same time as he.

Enthralled and speechless, Judy desired nothing more than to stand and stare, which she did, oblivious even of her husband. Her hands were clasped in front of her, her big eyes were wide and incredulous.

'I never believed I'd stand here,' she breathed rapturously at last. 'Oh, Chris—*thank* you for bringing me!'

A faint smile twisted his mouth; today he was the cool sardonic husband again and the tenderness of yesterday might have been a dream, elusive, fleeting—something that could not be recaptured, ever.

Ali Baba was speaking, talking about the Pharaohs of ancient Egypt and their deep concern with the after-life. He quoted Herodotus who estimated that one hundred thousand men had slaved for more than twenty years to build the Great Pyramid of Cheops. The stone was quarried from the Mokattam Hills and after being accurately shaped and dressed it was put into place, layer upon layer, until the Pyramid was completed. As he spoke Judy tipped back her head and stared upwards to the indescribable immensity of the man-made mountain soaring above her.

'It makes you feel like an ant,' she whispered to her husband. He nodded in agreement, glancing up himself but absorbed in what Ali Baba was saying.

'Monge, a mathematician employed by Napoleon, calculated that the masonry of the three largest Pyramids at Giza would make a wall, one foot thick, and ten feet high, long enough to surround the whole of France.'

Gasps were heard, but no one doubted this calculation. What did amaze people was the gullibility of the slaves of ancient Egypt. They would toil in this way for half a lifetime or more simply because they fully believed their ruler to be a god.

'Those who wish can now enter the grave,' Ali Baba was saying, and again Judy looked doubtfully at Chris. But he nodded and they made their way to the other side of the Pyramid. 'You'll have to bend, ladies and gentlemen,' said Ali Baba. 'And please hold on to the handrail.'

The passage was steep and long ... and certainly eerie, thought Judy, reaching out her other hand in an automatic gesture. Chris felt its warmth through his shirt and took it in his.

'All right?' he asked, half turning his head.

Judy nodded and smiled.

'It's creepy, though,' she said. 'How many years is it since Cheops was buried?'

'Five thousand; didn't you hear Ali Baba mention that?'

'I was looking—not listening,' she admitted. 'I must have missed a lot of what he said.'

They continued along a passage, lit by electricity, but no more than three feet high; Judy dared not think about the weight above, for to do so made her feel quite terrified. The Pharaoh's burial chamber was of black volcanic rock, his sarcophagus of red granite.

'It's ... weird,' quivered Judy, longing to be out in the sunlight again. It seemed almost like sacrilege for all these people to be in Cheops' funerary chamber.

A great sigh of relief left her lips when at last they were out in the light again.

One of the other Pyramids was built by Cheops' son, Chephren, and some of the people went into that too. But Chris and Judy wandered about among great granite blocks and slabs, the remains of temples which had been excavated after long centuries of being buried in the sand. And then they were gazing up at the Sphinx, which was close to the Chephren Pyramid. In Cheops' day the Sphinx was almost buried by sand; only its head gazed out over the vast desert, serene and inscrutable.

'You know,' murmured Judy smiling at Chris, 'I felt exactly like this the first time I stood on the Acropolis in Athens and looked at the Parthenon. You see the pictures of these famous places over and over again, and deep inside you there comes a longing that is really an ache, and it hurts awfully. Every time you see another picture the pain comes back and you say to yourself "I must see it—I *must*!" and then you start to—sort of—of—heave——'

'Good God, Judy,' broke in Chris, revolted. 'Spare me those sort of details, please!'

A tinkling laugh echoed through the clear warm air.

'I didn't mean I felt sick in the real sense of the word,' she began, when he again interrupted her.

'I'm relieved. Can we change the subject?'

Her laugh rang out again.

'I don't think I'm very good at describing my feelings, am I?'

'It just depends what your feelings were. I gained the impression you were suffering from some sort of malady.'

She stole a glance at him from under her lashes, sure he was teasing her. His face was set in unreadable lines. He appeared to be totally absorbed in the Sphinx. She fell silent, sharing his interest, taking her fill of the wonder of this colossal sandstone figure standing there on the plateau of Giza, where the Pharaohs who built these pyramids hoped to rest in peace. Strangely, though, scarcely any of them, no matter how great their ingenuity, had managed to beat the grave-robbers.

Ali Baba was talking again to those who had just come out of the Pyramid. There were English, Americans, French and Germans in the party and Ali Baba used the three languages in turn. He was an extremely highly educated man, and a philosopher. Chris and Judy joined the party and were in time to hear him talking about his wife. Someone asked if he ever took her out and he shook his head.

'She prefers to stay in,' he replied, and impulsively Judy said, not meaning her voice to carry to Ali Baba,

'They all say that! Ask a Cypriot why he doesn't take his wife out and he'll instantly say she prefers to stay in.'

Several heads turned, including Ali Baba's. His dark intelligent eyes moved slowly from Judy's flushed face to that of her husband.

'Often when I'm out with people like this,' he said, turning back to his audience, 'I talk about my wife and about the relationship we have. This leads always to a discussion in which all take part. And during this discussion I always ask the same question of the ladies. The response always interests me even though it never varies. Yes, I've asked the question to every nationality in the world, I think, and the response is always the same.'

Everyone was interested, especially the ladies, who were watching Ali Baba expectantly, waiting for the question. After a sidelong glance at Judy he smiled enigmatically and said, 'Ladies, if you are of the opinion that a husband should be the master then please raise your hands.'

The men were clearly amused, and curious, looking around, some with reluctant grins on their faces. Chris regarded his wife with an odd expression; Ali Baba sent her another glance as one hesitant hand was slowly raised. It had only required someone to make the first move and now every feminine hand except Judy's was raised. Judy bent her head, conscious of many eyes upon her, but more acutely aware that she most certainly was causing Chris embarrassment by not raising her hand. She seemed to be placing him in a position inferior to that of the other husbands present. Much as she regretted this she could not bring herself to raise her hand, and when she eventually looked up she was overwhelmingly relieved to see that all hands had now been lowered.

'Yes, ladies, that is the response I invariably receive. Of course, there are always the odd one or two who will not admit that they enjoy being mastered, and I noticed that today is no exception.' That was all, and Ali Baba did not look at Judy again.

What was Chris thinking? she wondered, unable to derive any information from his impassive countenance. She felt a surge of anger against Ali Baba, aware that his question was prompted by her retaliation to his assertion that his wife did not wish to go out with him.

But it was impossible to remain angry with him and when, a short while later he sought them out as they were wandering round the ruins of what had been massive buildings, Judy found herself unable to resist his smile.

'I was only teasing,' he assured her. But then he added, amusement in his eyes, 'You weren't honest, little lady—— No, do not interrupt, but listen to a wise old man for a moment. You are trying to deceive yourself, as many women do. You walk in the shadows because the fierce sunlight frightens you a little ... but don't remain in the shadows too long, my dear. The sun goes down, you know, and then there is complete darkness.' He reached out and patted her bare arm with a chubby, spotlessly clean hand. 'Go out to meet the sun, for assuredly if you don't it will move on ... to shed its warmth somewhere else.'

This rhetorical little speech stunned Judy for a moment. The man was omniscient! She glanced up at Chris; his unmoving countenance revealed nothing of his thoughts and yet all at once Judy saw him with Corinne, sitting at the far end of George's patio, and screened partly by the oleander bushes so that there was an intimacy in the scene which, Judy recalled, had made her furiously angry at the time. The sun would move on, Ali Baba had said ... 'to shed its warmth somewhere else'.

Fear touched Judy's heart. Was it already too late? Had she remained in the shadows too long? Ali Baba had wandered off, and urged by some magnetic force she stepped swiftly to her husband's side and took hold of his hand. Fear dropped from her like a cloak as his fingers curled round hers.

'What is it, little one?' He smiled down at her, but shook his head. 'Don't take Ali Baba too seriously; the sun always comes round again.'

Her face glowed.

'Chris....'

'My dear?'

She moistened her lips.

'What I'm trying to say is—is...' Again her voice trailed away and his mouth curved in amusement.

'What is it that you find so difficult to say?' He had begun to walk on, over the hot sand towards the place where the ponies and traps were waiting to take them back to the coach. 'Can I be of any assistance?'

She laughed then ... but the moment was lost and she merely said,

'You're kind, Chris—and understanding.'

A small sigh and then,

'Kind, am I? And understanding....' He released her hand, increasing his pace at the same time so that she had to skip now and then to keep up with him.

They sat side by side in the trap, neither speaking a word. Chris's face was set and his chin thrust forward. He had drifted from her and she felt chilled. But with the resilience of youth she rallied, turning her head to look back at the picture postcard scene of the Pyramids and Sphinx, standing as they had stood for centuries and centuries, under a blue electric sky from which the sun blazed down on to the arid, burning desert.

The pony began to trot and Judy twisted round again. The coach was there, the driver in his seat, waiting. There were other coaches, too, with people pouring from them. Camels waited, often emitting the weirdest sounds, to carry the more venturesome sightseers up to the Pyramids. There were the ponies and traps, with dusky Arabs at the ponies' heads; there were the Arab hawkers, and the ubiquitous dragomans who would —for a fee, of course—recite parrot-fashion the historical narrative that had been passed down from father to son for generations. There were the places where refreshments could be bought, there were eager children talking to the smiling camel-drivers. It was exciting, although rather overcrowded. For Judy it was the fulfilment of a dream and she sighed contentedly when, a little while later, they were in the coach and driving back to the hotel for lunch.

The afternoon was spent in the museum, the major attraction naturally being the Tutankhamen Gallery. On either side of the entrance stood a man-sized figure carved in ebony. Skirts of gold encircled their loins, golden sandals were on their feet and on their foreheads they wore magnificent gold headdresses. They had guarded Tutankhamen's tomb, standing erect and holding staffs on the top of which were golden balls.

Facing the entrance was an ebony figure of the ancient Egyptian deity, the god Anubis, conductor of the dead, the ears of his jackal's head cocked and alert.

The fantastic grave furniture included golden chariots, chairs, beds, chests and divans. The jewellery of the Pharaoh filled case after case and in one room stood the magnificent golden casket in which the body of the king lay when it was found in the tomb in the famous Valley of the Kings. And of course there was the incredibly beautiful mask of the king in gold and lapis lazuli which had covered the head of Tutankhamen's embalmed body.

'I feel completely dazzled,' exclaimed Judy as they came out of the museum. 'Have you ever experienced anything like it in all your life?'

'Never. It was a good idea of yours to suggest coming to Egypt.'

'You're glad?' His admission had made her happy. She was glad he had used the word 'suggest'. It had begun to trouble her that he had come simply in order to pander to her wishes.

'Yes, Judy, I'm glad.'

On the way back to the hotel his manner of cool disinterest fell from him and he drew Judy's arm through his as they sat close together in the coach.

'Oh, look!' exclaimed Judy as they passed a mud-brick village some distance from the road. 'They use buffaloes here where in Cyprus they use donkeys.'

The blindfold water buffalo was tethered to a primitive water-wheel, sadly treading an endless circle. In Cyprus donkeys were used in this way, but only in the very remote villages.

'Poor thing!' cried the woman behind. 'What a life!'

But the animals were well fed and appeared to be healthy. True, the camels in their train often grumbled and a donkey would occasionally send out a cry of complaint.

Farther along they passed three gaily clad women with earthenware pitchers balanced gracefully on their heads, going to draw water. There were flashes of white teeth in dusky faces as the women smiled and waved to the occupants of the coach.

'How do they do it?' someone asked incredulously. 'Just look at that one. The pitcher's enormous!'

'And it isn't even upright. How they can balance them in a sideways position like that beats me!'

'It beats me how they can balance them at all!'

Yet to the women it was no trouble. They learned from being small children and balancing these heavy vessels on their heads was almost part of their education.

On arrival at the hotel there was the rather sad parting between Ali Baba and his group of tourists. Although typical of the kind of man who escorted parties of tourists on their various trips in and around Cairo, Ali Baba possessed something more than the mere ability to share his knowledge. He was more than a guide; many of the tourists felt that had they known him just a few more days he would have become a friend. He was a deep thinker, and yet he could joke himself and laugh at the jokes of others. To both Judy and Chris the memory of Cairo would always be the memory of Ali Baba, and they suspected this would be the case with hundreds of other tourists whose good fortune it was to meet this wonderful man.

'Remember what I said about the sun,' he twinkled as he shook hands with Judy. And then, to Chris, 'I declared that you were a lucky man, sir, and I repeat that. Take care of this delectable child!'

'That is my intention,' smiled Chris, and held out his hand. 'Goodbye, Ali Baba, I sincerely hope we shall meet again some day.'

CHAPTER NINE

WITHIN a fortnight of returning from the cruise Judy was having her birthday party. Chris had been away in Athens—on business, he said—for the past week, but he had promised to be back for her birthday. The Palmers were invited to the party, as also was George. To Judy's disgust Chris told her to invite Corinne Moore. This request placed Judy in a quandary. If she refused to invite Corinne, Chris might conclude that her refusal stemmed from jealousy. If she did invite the girl then the evening would assuredly be ruined for Judy because Corinne would repeat her performance and monopolize Chris for most of the time.

'I don't care for Corinne very much,' she ventured, hoping that might just be sufficient to make her husband drop the matter. But he frowned and said,

'She's an old friend of mine. It would be the height of bad manners to exclude her. Besides, George is coming and they're living in the same house. It would embarrass him to have to come without her.'

A determined light entered Judy's eyes. She forgot everything except her original intention of attaining equality with Chris.

'It's my party and I can invite whom I like. I'm not inviting Corinne.'

A metallic glint in his eyes, a compression of his mouth. He stared down at her with fine arrogance from his superior height.

'You appear to have misunderstood me,' came his soft words after a silence which robbed Judy of much of her confidence. 'I said—Corinne is an old friend of mine.'

A quarrel could have ensued, had Judy persisted in her refusal, but a coldness would have remained between her and Chris and this she could not bear. In any case, she had a shrewd suspicion that, no matter how prolonged her stand, she would in the end have been forced to submit to her husband's will.

. Judy saw that George and Floria sat together at the table. By the same planning she saw that Corinne was as far away from Chris as possible. In fact, with a sudden little surge of spite she put the English girl next to Vincent. If Chris noticed this last deliberate move he gave nothing away. He talked to his mother for a good deal of the time; Judy noticed that there was a seriousness about their faces and a certain gravity in their tones, although she could not catch a word of what was being said, no matter how she strained her ears.

The meal over, they strayed out in twos and threes to the verandah where Spiros served the coffee. Chris was with his mother and after they had walked along to a shadowed spot, sheltered by vines growing along a trellis and encroaching on to the roof, they both sat down. Judy frowned in puzzlement and curiosity. There was some mystery, she felt sure, especially as on one occasion as she caught the older woman's eyes she had seen an unnatural brightness there.

Judy and Corinne had not met since she and Chris had returned from the cruise and on finding a place next to Judy Corinne asked how she had enjoyed herself.

'It was most pleasant, thank you,' coldly came the reply. Judy reached for her coffee cup and raised it to her lips. Corinne smiled faintly, musing a while before she spoke again.

'It was the idea of visiting Egypt that attracted you,

George told me.'

Judy listened to the night sounds—the crickets and sheep bells, the distant barking of a dog and the familiar cry of a donkey on the lonely moonlit hillside. The north-west wind blew up from the sea, warmed by the heat which the water had stolen from the sun. Carried on this breeze was the exotic perfume gathered from the flowers blooming in profusion in the hillside gardens.

'I've always wanted to visit Egypt, yes.' Still quite cool was her voice, but Judy turned now, to look at her companion. 'It more than came up to my expectations,' she added with a touch of well-aimed malice, for Judy was caught by a desire to make the girl jealous, if that were at all possible. Perhaps, though, this type of woman was never jealous. Floria had hinted that had Corinne played her cards right Chris would have married her. But Corinne had not played her cards right; she had succumbed to Chris's persuasions ... and that had put an end to any chance she might have had regarding marriage. So now Corinne was probably resigned, knowing she could still make good use of that 'enormous attraction' which she had for Chris.

'I should find it a dead bore myself,' frowned Corinne. 'Tombs and ruins and museums are not in my line. I expect poor old Chris was bored, but of course he'd hide that fact. There's one thing more than any other which I adore about Chris—his manners are impeccable.'

Judy reddened with disgust. The girl had neither tact nor sensibility. She spoke in the manner of one whose intimacy with Chris was common knowledge. In view of this Judy saw no reason for holding her own thrust and she said in cutting tones,

'You did not learn from him, apparently.'

An astounded silence followed, cut through at length

by the rather strident voice of Jean Palmer, talking to Vincent, whose obese body reclined ungracefully in a low wicker armchair.

'Are you insinuating,' muttered Corinne between her teeth, 'that *my* manners are *not* impeccable?'

Judy measured her with a scathing glance.

'They're far from impeccable. In fact, you appear to have forgotten you're talking to Chris's wife.'

Another moment of silence, and then, in a voice tinged with the soft guttural threat from an animal's throat,

'Be careful, Judy. I'm all for freedom in marriage and I think it's good for husband and wife to have a change now and then. But Chris might not be of the same mind....' Corinne sent Judy a narrowed, significant glance which was designed to convey more than words but which, on the contrary, only succeeded in bringing a blank expression to Judy's face. 'Make an enemy of me, Judy, and you'll regret it for a very long while.' Corinne broke into a smile, but there was no humour on her face as she added, 'You know what I'm talking about, so there's no need for that dazed and uncomprehending look.'

'I haven't the faintest idea what you're talking about.' A husband and wife should have a change now and then.... The girl spoke in riddles.

A short laugh fell from Corinne's lips. It attracted the attention of both Jean and Keith Palmer, but for the moment neither Judy nor Corinne noticed.

'Your little escapade when Chris was away in Athens——'

'My——?' Judy gaped at her. 'What did you say?'

'Such well-feigned innocence,' sneered Corinne, all efforts at politeness dropped. 'I happened to see you and George—oh no, don't look so startled; I haven't said a word either to him or to Chris. But be careful

161

how you treat me, or I might choose to tell Chris of this little affair going on between you and George——'

'Corinne, I must apologize for neglecting you.' Chris's deep rich voice broke in on the conversation; he smiled charmingly at Corinne and sat down close to her. But as his glance strayed to his wife's face he said sharply,

'What is it, Judy? Are you unwell?'

She swallowed the little ball of fear that had lodged in her throat. Floria and George. . . . Corinne must have seen them together somewhere, and it must have been dark, otherwise Corinne would not have thought it was Judy she had seen.

'No—I'm f-fine. If you'll excuse me——' And without any further explanation Judy rose and left them, going over to Floria and sitting down beside her. Yet having made this determined move Judy was at a loss as to how she should handle the situation. But there was only one course open to her, she decided after the minimum of thought. There was neither the time nor the need for diplomacy and she came straight to the point.

'I've just been talking to Corinne——'

'I saw you.' Floria's eyes were on the wide doorway leading from the patio to the sitting-room. George was standing in the aperture, talking to Madam Voulis. 'I thought you didn't like her.'

'I detest her. Floria, she's seen you and George somewere together——'

'She's——!' The colour drained from Floria's face. But she recovered somewhat almost immediately and said, 'She couldn't have. We've only met at night...' And then her voice faded as she realized what she had admitted.

'Floria . . . have you been seeing George regularly?'

The Greek girl nodded unhappily.

'Yes, Judy. After having those two days together we both knew we really loved one another—we knew before then,' she told Judy. 'But those two days really brought us together.' She stopped, her eyes filling up, and Judy said, her voice choked and husky,

'Where have you been meeting?'

'In the arbour.'

'The arbour?' frowned Judy. 'You don't mean here—in our garden?' and when Floria again nodded, 'Are you crazy? In the garden—*this* garden!—with Vincent in the house? Are you crazy?' she repeated, staring at Floria in amazement.

'He never goes to bed early, but he thought I did. Instead, I went to meet George in the garden.'

Judy shook her head, unable to take in this utter lack of care.

'George ... couldn't he see the danger?'

'There wasn't any danger. Vincent never walks in the garden. He's too busy with the bottle. George came up each night and I met him in the arbour. There's a gap in the hedge, as you know, and he entered the garden that way. It's a great distance from the house.' She stopped and frowned. 'Did Corinne see us in the arbour?' she asked, forgetting she had just asserted that Corinne had not seen them together.

'She must have done,' returned Judy reflectively. 'That's why she concluded that it was me.'

'You?' Floria knitted her brows questioningly.

'Corinne thinks it's George and I who are having an affair.'

'She said so? She tackled you with it?' For the moment Floria was diverted from the more serious matter of her own position. 'She wouldn't do that, surely?'

'Corinne will say whatever she's a mind to say. She threatened to tell Chris of my—affair if I didn't treat her with civility.' Judy paused thoughtfully. 'How did she come to be in our garden, I wonder?'

'That's what I've been pondering. She's a great walker and often strolls about the lanes at night. And one evening I did think I'd heard someone, because it frightened me. I couldn't speak for fear, but George was so kind and—soothing. He just held me and we sat there, very quietly, but we concluded that I'd been mistaken because we didn't hear anyone wandering about either in the garden or in the lane outside.'

Judy became thoughtful again.

'I think I can see it all,' she murmured at last. 'She must have been walking along the lane and heard George's voice on the other side of the hedge. Naturally she'd be curious, and she must have entered the garden through the gap, just as George was accustomed to doing. That was what you heard. She would then stand still and quiet, listening. You say you didn't speak?' Judy stopped, waiting for a response and the Greek girl nodded. 'George spoke, though, so you said. So she would naturally conclude that he was speaking to me.' Judy looked at her sister-in-law. 'There were only two girls who could be there in George's arms— you or I. As she would instantly conclude that it couldn't be you, because your husband was in the house, she decided it was I who was having an affair with George.'

'What will she do?' asked Floria, her face still very white. 'You said she threatened to tell Chris?'

'No——' Judy shook her head. 'She said she'd tell him if I wasn't careful how I treated her. You see, I'd just been rather uncivil to her—only in retaliation for something she had said, though. However, it aroused her anger and she then went on to inform me that she knew of the "little affair" I was having with George.' It would be amusing were it not so serious from Floria's

164

point of view, thought Judy, smiling faintly to herself. 'Can you remember what George said to you that night—when you were scared by this sound, I mean?'

'He just said "Hush, darling. Don't tremble so. I'm here, and I love you." ' Floria's colour rose as she spoke, but she seemed to feel she owed it to Judy to offer an adequate answer to her question. 'What was the outcome?' added Floria. 'You didn't tell her it was I, obviously.'

'Chris came up and interrupted us. I realized that Corinne had seen you and George together, so I wasted no time in coming to you.'

Floria looked at Judy, scared and trembling.

'You're going to tell her it wasn't you?'

Judy shook her head.

'For the present, no. I'll try to get her into conversation again and see what else I can learn. But I don't think she intends mentioning the matter to Chris——'

'Why, I wonder? She's a spiteful cat and I could rather imagine her running straight to Chris and giving you away, especially as she's so crazy about him herself. I should have thought she'd seize upon such a wonderful opportunity to blacken your name.' Floria's voice was edged with fear. 'If she does, you'll have to tell Chris the truth, in order to clear your own name, and he'll tell Vincent...' Her voice quivered away to nothing and tears started to her eyes. 'I wish I were dead,' she whispered distractedly. 'Oh, Judy, what is to become of me?'

'Don't cry, Floria,' pleaded Judy. 'And don't worry too much. I'll not give you away, I promise.'

'But you'll have to!'

'Corinne didn't seem at all inclined to put Chris in possession of the facts—no, like you, I don't know the reason, and, like you, I'm puzzled. However, for the present you're safe and so am I.' Judy looked straight at her. 'But don't take any more risks, Floria. Please promise me, for I don't want to see you in trouble.'

'I promise——' Floria burst into tears. 'I don't know h-how we can go b-back to being acquaintances, b-but we m-must.' A handkerchief was dragged from her pocket and she hastily dried her eyes, casting a swift look round to see if anyone had noticed her breakdown. 'I wanted to have an affair with George—but it isn't possible, is it?'

Judy shook her head, fingering away her own tears.

'No, Floria, it isn't possible.' It would also be fruitless, and would in time become unsatisfying, but naturally Judy saw no necessity for mentioning this.

'You can't let Corinne go on thinking an awful thing like that about you,' cried Floria as the thought registered at last. 'No, you can't! Judy, I'm—I'm in dreadful trouble, aren't I?'

'Of course you're not. I'm willing to leave things as they are, so stop worrying.'

'You're so kind. I don't know how to thank you——' Floria shook her head. 'No, I can't think of words to express my gratitude.'

'Then don't try,' returned Judy, wishing only to end this dismal conversation.

'You've saved me from——' Floria's eyes wandered to the table farther along where her husband sprawled inelegantly on a chair, his short legs stretched out in front of him. 'Who can say what you've saved me from?'

'Forget all about it,' advised Judy in soothing tones. 'It's all over and done with and we should be thankful that Corinne has got us mixed up.' At that moment George came out and joined them. Madam Voulis had gone over to join the Palmers and Floria said, speaking to George,

'Has Mother been talking about Father?'

166

George looked puzzled.

'Your father? No, why should she?'

'He wants to come back to her.'

Judy stared, wondering again what her father-in-law was like.

'Is she intending taking him back?'

'I think she'll let Chris advise her. They've been talking the matter over this evening; I watched them. I think Mother will have Father back.'

'Does your mother care for him?' The words came hesitantly, for Judy was disinclined to intrude into personal affairs. Yet at the same time she felt she should exhibit some degree of interest.

'She loves him. Theirs wasn't an arranged marriage. They met at the house of a mutual friend and fell in love.' Floria's voice contained a hint of anger; it was not difficult to guess that she was condemning her father for arranging her own marriage when he and her mother had chosen their own partners.

'Will he come here—if she takes him back?'

'I expect so. We all spend the whole of the summer here with Chris—always have.'

Vincent came out and sat close to Judy. His hand moved unnecessarily on to the arm of her chair, then she felt his hot fingers on her wrist. Swiftly she removed her hand, but with the persistence of his type Vincent then moved his leg so that it touched hers.

'Will you all excuse me?' Judy rose as she spoke, hoping her tones were not too unpleasant. 'I'm neglecting the Palmers....'

Both Jean and Keith gave her odd glances as she joined them, and only then did Judy begin to wonder if they had heard anything Corinne said. Obviously they had, because Jean baldly asked Judy about the 'little escapade' Corinne had mentioned. There was a teasing light in Jean's eye, but to Judy's relief there was

167

nothing else and Judy managed effectively to pass over the matter, saying it was a joke of Corinne's.

But Judy felt a surge of anger against the English girl; she also felt the strain of the past few minutes and a desire for solitude assailed her. After talking politely to the Palmers for a few minutes she went off on her own into the garden. The night-scents were heady, the air soft and still. A moon hung in the sky, but it was cut into by a wedge of the mountain which detracted from its light. She sat down under a tree and allowed her mind to dwell on Floria's plight. There seemed no future for her—just a long unhappy trek with the shadow of George in the unreachable distance and the very real figure of Vincent walking beside her.

A sudden check was put upon Judy's musings as a slim dark figure approached. Corinne.... She saw Judy and sat down on the bench beside her.

'What's this?—a desire for solitude?'

'What do you want?' asked Judy sharply, ignoring the sneering accents in which the question was put.

'I saw you come out and thought you might like to continue our interesting conversation. You see, just before Chris interrupted us I gained the impression that you were intending to bluff.' No comment from Judy and Corinne went on, 'It would be quite useless, because I saw the pair of you with my own eyes.'

'In the arbour?' Judy was curious to know whether or not her deductions were correct.

'In the arbour.' A small pause and then, 'Obviously you're used to meeting George in the arbour?'

Judy allowed that question to pass unanswered.

'You're very sure it was me you saw.'

'Certainly I'm sure.' Corinne's voice was slightly raised; Judy could almost see the accompanying lift of her delicately pencilled brows. 'Who else would be allowing George to make love to her? And it wasn't the first time, was it, not by any means?'

'You saw me on more than one occasion?' queried Judy. Floria had heard a sound only on one occasion—or so she said.

'I didn't see you on more than one occasion, no. But what about the night you stole away from the rest of us and went into the house with George?' Judy remained silent, for a tingling of fear assailed her. Supposing Corinne were not intending to keep quiet? Judy would be faced with a terrible decision. Either she must expose Floria, who would then be in the most dire trouble, or she herself must be in trouble with Chris. And recalling that terrifying scene when Chris had discovered she had been meeting Ronnie, Judy shivered in her shoes, all her ideas of 'man-management' rapidly disappearing.

'Did you come into the garden?' inquired Judy at last, again desirous of learning if her deductions had been correct.

'Naturally I was curious when on taking a walk along the lane I heard George's voice uttering the most passionate love phrases. There was a gap in the hedge, so I stepped through——'

'So you were intent on prying,' cut in Judy, her tones vibrant with disgust.

'I've just said it was interest, but you can call it what you like,' added Corinne with a laugh. 'Here was George, in Chris's garden, and with Chris away in Athens ...' Corinne's voice tailed off. She seemed to be chuckling inwardly now, as if the whole thing were one huge joke. 'I must admit I admire your courage, for Chris can be a nasty piece of work—but perhaps you've not met up with that side of him yet. However, as I was saying, I stepped through the Ledge, and there you were, all cosily in the shadows, your head romantically nestling into his broad shoulder, and George de-

169

claring his love, with you a rapt listener, not saying one single word.' Corinne's laugh rang out again and Judy flushed as if the guilt had actually been hers and not her sister-in-law's.

'So I was right in everything,' murmured Judy to herself.

'What did you say?'

'Nothing that would interest you.' The words were curtly spoken and Corinne's sudden anger could be sensed. Judy turned her head, but the shadows hid her companion's expression. 'You—you gave me to understand you—didn't intend telling my husband....' Judy spoke with difficulty, almost unable to articulate words which pronounced her own guilt.

'I'm no spoilsport,' returned Corinne with a chuckle. 'I know you dislike me intensely, and I don't particularly like you, but as I said earlier, I consider it is good for a husband and wife to have a change.' Something indefinable in her words troubled Judy and presently she said,

'Are there ... conditions?'

'Obviously. And that's the real reason why I sought you out here, in the garden.' The flow of Corinne's tongue was smooth now ... but again that soft guttural noise could be detected. 'You will be left free to indulge in your affair with George so long as you leave me free to conduct mine with Chris.' Corinne crossed her shapely legs in the dark; the movement was neither swift nor sudden and yet Judy jumped. Her nerves must be pretty frayed, she concluded, beginning to feel quite drained by what she had been through during the past half hour or so. She knew her face was white, and her heart was heavy, because it seemed that Chris was indeed having an affair with Corinne, even though he was now married, and Judy was overwhelmed with the tragic conviction that it was all her fault. Chris was a Greek and Greek men were virile and passionate. She had known this, and yet had persisted in her endeavours to bring some affection into her relationship with Chris before agreeing to put their marriage on a normal footing. Chris had not waited—could not wait....

Tears pricked Judy's eyes. She had lost him, she concluded despairingly, and all through her own silly efforts to manage him and her striving for equality. She had stayed in the shadows too long, and now the sun had moved round to shed its warmth elsewhere. If only she had taken more notice of Ali Baba—but she had tried, she recalled. It had been shyness on her part, not any longer an insistence on getting to know Chris better, which in the end had kept them apart. And, with the inconsistency of woman, Judy experienced a surge of anger against her husband. He should have known she was shy, should have been firmer and more manly; he should have asserted himself right from the start, insisting on his rights. And then he would not have been forced to go back to Corinne.

The tears fell, tears of anger and hopelessness; and disappointment that her husband was a weakling, and not masterful as she now knew she wanted him to be. Ali Baba was right when he said she had not been honest. But what was the use wanting to be mastered when she had a husband like Chris? Judy frowned suddenly. He had been masterful on occasions, though, now she came to think of it. What about that scene over Ronnie? That had been rather too dramatic, really. She didn't want to be terrified ... no, just made to feel a little apprehensive of her husband, as she had on the one or two other occasions when he had decided to assert his authority.

Judy's frown deepened. What a contradictory character he was! Would she ever understand him? But why ask that, when she had now lost him altogether?

171

Her tragic reflections were interrupted by Corinne's soft and silky accents inquiring the reason for this long silence.

'The matter doesn't require thought,' Corinne added. 'Promise to be a little helpful, and in turn I shall keep silent about you and George.'

'Helpful?'

A small silence, broken only by the soft echo of laughter coming from the great drawing-room of Salaris House. The windows were wide open, for the night was warm and balmy and intoxicatingly perfumed.

'You'll not be possessive where Chris is concerned. You'll turn a blind eye when he goes off for a week-end. And you yourself could on occasions take yourself off to Cyprus. I'm sure you miss your grandfather—as he must miss you.'

Judy felt quite sick.

'You're disgusting!' she cried. 'Have you no sense of decency?'

An incredulous little laugh reminded Judy of something she had quite forgotten: she herself was supposed to be having an affair with George.

'I like that! Who are you to adopt the righteously indignant manner? You really are the limit, Judy!' exclaimed Corinne with another incredulous little laugh. 'Mind you, it does puzzle me that you can so shamelessly indulge in an affair after the strictness with which you've been brought up——' she stopped. 'Did you hear anything?' she inquired after a moment.

Judy shook her head in the darkness.

'No—did you?'

'I was probably mistaken. However, I'm going back —but remember what I've said. No possessiveness where Chris is concerned. He was mine before he was yours, always remember that. And,' added Corinne

172

with emphasis, 'see that you treat me with respect. No
cy disdain from now on. I'm just as good as you are,
and you'll keep that in mind or else...' That was all.
Judy stemmed the rising fury within her for, far from
reating Corinne with respect, she could at this moment have turned around and soundly slapped her
face.

CHAPTER TEN

ON returning to the patio the two girls found it deserted except for Floria, who was still sitting in the chair, tapping one hand absently on the table in front of her.

'Is everyone inside?' Corinne glanced towards the open doorway of the drawing-room. 'All drinking,' she laughed. 'I must join them!'

'You've been crying,' observed Floria anxiously as Judy sat down on the opposite side of the table. 'What's wrong?' Her glance flickered to Corinne's quickly disappearing figure. 'Has she been upsetting you?'

Judy hesitated. How long could she allow Corinne to go on thinking she was unfaithful to Chris? The girl would snigger each time they met; she would broach the subject often, Judy felt sure . . . she might even want to discuss it, as, no doubt, she would discuss her affair with Chris. Floria was waiting breathlessly for her reply and Judy's heart sank within her. She could not ask Floria to confess.

'No—it's nothing——' She broke off, giving a sigh of relief as Madam Voulis joined them, a smile on her face which Judy had never seen before. She spoke at once, to them both, as she glanced from one to the other in turn.

'Father and I are going to live together again. He has asked me to forgive him and to try again. I'm taking Chris's advice and taking him back.'

Judy did not know what to say; Floria on the other hand smiled at her mother and said she was glad.

Madam Voulis then glanced questioningly at her daughter-in-law and Judy felt she had to say something, although she fumbled for words and even when she did manage to speak she felt shy and embarrassed.

'I'm glad, Mother—if it will make you happy, that is.'

'It will make me happy. Both Michalis and I have been stubborn, but we're older now and, I hope, wiser. I don't know if Chris has told you, but we've been parted for over five years.'

Judy nodded.

'He did tell me, yes.'

A silence fell between them and eventually Madam Voulis said good night and went inside. She could be heard saying her good nights all around and a short while later her bedroom light was switched on, throwing its amber glow on to the lawn.

'Mother was generous when she said they both were stubborn,' commented Floria after a while. 'Father's very much like Chris—haughty and superior and very domineering—or at least he was. Mother's travelled around and seen how women should live, how they should be treated by their husbands. From the first she tried to—well, to mould Father, I suppose is how one might put it. But he was stubborn, insisting on adhering to the customs of the East. A husband should be like a god, was his idea, and even though, when we were small, Mother threatened to go when we were older, he still remained arrogant and domineering. Mother did not have a happy life because she couldn't be content with that sort of subjugation which Greek women normally accept. The marriage was really on the rocks from the beginning...' Her voice trailed away as a strange light entered her eyes. She looked across at Judy and as the full truth hit her she gave a little gasp. 'I see it all now! I've been puzzled by

Chris's attitude with you; I couldn't understand why he should be so—soft, and so obliging, allowing you all your own way—but it's as plain as can be; he doesn't intend letting his marriage go the same way——' Floria broke off and then added, 'I always thought he loved you, waiting all that time, and I'm sure of it now.' She gave a smothered little laugh. 'Just listen to *me* telling *you* that my brother loves you. You know, of course—always have done.'

Love.... Judy realized she was trembling all over. Chris loved her? And yet wasn't it feasible? Two years he had waited—over two years. And how could it be desire, she asked herself again, when he had never attempted to take her? How could she have been so blind? And to think—— Ashamedly Judy checked her thoughts, but they were insistently clamouring for attention. To think she had assumed he had gone back to Corinne, because he now no longer desired the girl he had chosen for his wife. Judy tugged at the little lace collar of her dress, which seemed to be choking her. She had suspected him of all that was bad when in reality he was wonderful. She had only a short while ago branded him a weakling, because he had not asserted his rights. He had been treading warily, she saw that now, and Judy spoke her thoughts aloud when presently she said, shades of contrition in her voice,

'He intended learning a lesson from the break-up of his parents' marriage....'

'Yes; that's obvious. Women today are fighting for equality and if men are wise they accept that women are in fact equals in all but physical strength. Only where a wife is a partner can real happiness dominate the marriage. My father wouldn't have this, but he must have promised to reform or Mother wouldn't be taking him back.' Floria paused broodingly. 'His last act of true domination was in coercing me into marriage with Vincent. Mother and he had a dreadful quarrel over that.'

Judy looked at Floria in some puzzlement.

'You were living with your mother at the time?'

Floria nodded.

'You're going to say that I needn't have married Vincent?'

'Yes, that's what I was going to say. You were with your mother and you could have remained with her.'

'Father said if I didn't obey him he would cut all of us off without a penny; he would also stop Mother's allowance.'

'I still don't understand. Surely Chris would have looked after you both?'

A long silence ensued, for the Greek girl seemed reluctant to speak. However, eventually she did, to say that, at the time, Chris possessed all his father's arrogant belief in the inferiority of women, and he agreed entirely with the system of arranged marriages. He had been a party to the coercion, but Floria firmly believed he was now sorry and that had he his time to come over again he would certainly not listen to the offer of a man Floria did not love.

Judy thought a long while about this. She herself had gained the impression that Chris was sorry for his sister in spite of his once having said, with what appeared to be heartless unconcern,

'A woman should be satisfied with her husband, no matter what he's like.' And later on he had appeared even more heartless when he had observed that Floria's husband would most likely beat her.

Chris probably felt that the damage was done and as it could not be undone Floria must endeavour to resign herself to her fate.

As the slow minutes passed and Judy continued to muse on what Floria had said she remembered a remark Chris had made to her grandfather. Chris had said he hoped Judy had been brought up to know her place as he wasn't expecting to have to deal with a rebellious wife. At that time, then, he had not intended allowing his wife much of her own way, evidently. And yet he had loved her—if Floria's deductions were correct, and Judy was now quite sure they were. Yes, he had offered because he loved her, but at that time he was still imbued with the idea of male superiority. But it would appear that his love had been so great that he was not taking the slightest risk. He wanted Judy for ever, and so he was willing to let her 'manage' him, and he was also willing to wait until she herself had decided that management was complete. Would he always be so obliging? A wry smile hovered on Judy's lips and unconsciously she shook her head from side to side. . . .

She could not find him anywhere. Impatiently she inquired of George where he was.

'He was going off down the garden the last time I saw him,' smiled George, all unaware of what Floria would eventually tell him when an opportunity came for them to be alone. 'He's an excellent host, but he gets tired of the babble and goes off now and then for a moment of peace and quiet. Always was like that, but we understand him. Should be back directly.' George had not been looking at Judy and when, on finishing speaking, he did glance at her his eyes opened wide in consternation. 'You're as white as a sheet. Is anything wrong?'

'No—no, of course not.' But Judy's heart thumped. Chris was in the garden. . . . 'When did he go?' she eventually quivered.

George frowned in puzzlement.

'He's been gone about fifteen minutes. Is it important what time he went?'

Judy shook her head, mumbled an almost inaudible, 'Excuse me,' and left George standing there in the drawing-room, staring after her before turning to speak a friendly but impersonal few words to the lovely girl standing some little distance away from him.

Corinne had stopped speaking, to ask Judy if she had heard anything.... This incident occupied Judy's mind to the exclusion of all else as she stepped out on to the patio. Fifteen minutes. Yes, Chris would certainly have been in the garden when Corinne was asking that question. Had he heard anything? 'I must look for him—even i-if he h-has heard....' She must know at once. It was as if she were being drawn out to the garden. But she *must know*—immediately!

And she did, without going in search of Chris. He appeared at the end of the patio and began to cover its long length, slowly, his eyes never leaving Judy's face. Stark savagery burned in those dark eyes and his lips were drawn back almost in a snarl. He and Judy were alone on the patio, he advancing towards her and she automatically taking backward steps, vaguely aware that someone had pushed the big doors to, so that the people in the drawing-room were now quite separate from the two outside. Still Chris came towards her and Judy continued to move away, with a sort of strategic panic, towards the vine-covered trellis at the far end, while her brain worked furiously in an endeavour to find words with which to answer him when he should at last decide to break this terrifying silence. What must she do? she asked herself feverishly. She could not expose Floria ... but ... was he intending to murder her? wondered Judy, choking with fear. Fleetingly she lived again through that scene over Ronnie; she had thought she would collapse with fright, but what she had experienced then was a mere fluttering of nerves in comparison to this. If only her heart wouldn't thump so; it made her feel quite sick and for one wild moment she thought she must blurt out the truth. But she managed to check the impulse at the same time as coming to a physical halt as the backs of her legs touched the vines.

'Chris...' She just had to speak, even though she knew she could find little to add to that huskily-spoken word. 'You were in the—in the g-garden?'

He made no answer to that as he came to a halt, very close, so that he towered above her, threatening and pale with fury.

'So you're trembling, are you?' he said through gritting teeth. 'But, by God, that's nothing to what you will be when I've finished with you. Affair with George, eh——?' He broke off, unable, it seemed, to speak for the smouldering wrath in which he was totally enveloped. Judy put a shaking hand to her heart; her own lips moved, but soundlessly. 'I'll strangle you! I'll break every bone in your body! Get into the house—up to your room—at once!' He swallowed thickly as if endeavouring to free his throat from the ball of fire that was lodging there. 'Ten minutes from now you'll wish you were dead!' He meant it, too, she had no doubt of that, and Judy knew she could not continue shielding Floria. Yet the words that would save her and condemn her sister-in-law would not come. No, she couldn't expose Floria—not until she had spoken to her.

'I w-want to sp-speak to Floria,' she began, but was immediately interrupted.

'I ordered you into the house! Do you go or do I drag you there?'

But Judy was unable to take one single step. Sheer terror possessed her even as her husband was possessed

180

by a white-hot fury. His eyes burned into her like an all-consuming flame and she wished only for some sort of merciful oblivion to descend upon her. Vaguely through the paralysing fear of her mind emerged the conclusions she had formed so short a time ago. Chris loved her and had pandered to her only as a sort of insurance for a happy life with her. He had allowed her to believe she was managing him and attaining equality. Yes, he had always known what she was about and yet he had observed it with amused indulgence. All this suggested softness and understanding ... but ... Looking at him now, with murder in his eyes, she could not believe he possessed one atom of softness—or of mercy.

'Chris,' she faltered, extending a hand towards him. 'If you will call your sister——' She broke off, feeling she must surely collapse with relief as the doors to the drawing-room were flung wide and Keith Palmer and George came rushing out, followed by everyone else.

'Chris!' It was Keith who spoke, for the others seemed completely dazed. 'Chris—it's Vincent. He's—he's...' He could not continue, but George managed to explain that Vincent had suddenly slumped in his chair, uttered just one little groan of pain, and when Keith ran to him he was dead.

'Dead?' Chris stared. 'Dead?' he repeated, unable to take it in.

'I couldn't believe it at first,' Keith was saying, but Judy went to Floria and, putting her arm around her, led her away from the chatter and consternation, and into a small sitting-room which Judy and Chris favoured when they were alone.

Floria was dry-eyed and dazed and for a long while they both sat there, each trying not to dwell on what this sudden death would mean. At last Floria's unnatural restraint broke and she sobbed uncontrollably on Judy's breast.

'I wanted him to die ... oh, Judy, I'm wicked—wicked!'

'Darling, you have no control over such things——'

'I wanted him dead!' interrupted Floria wildly. 'You're not listening, Judy. I wished him dead—I prayed for it!'

'Nothing you did could have caused this—this disaster.' Judy spoke softly and soothingly, her hand automatically stroking Floria's hair. 'These things are not in our hands,' she went on practically. 'And you mustn't blame yourself for anything—hush, Floria, don't sob like this! You mustn't feel guilty—you must not!' A slight sharpness touched Judy's voice; she experienced an unreasoning anger that Floria should be troubled by conscience. She had suffered at Vincent's hands when he was alive and now, it seemed, she was to be plagued by a guilt that was going to mar her chances of happiness later, when she and George were able to marry. 'You were never unfaithful to Vincent——'

'I was, in my mind—oh, many times!' Sobs shook Floria's body again and Judy just held her close, thinking that Vincent had been unfaithful many times too —and not merely in his mind.

Chris entered the room, accompanied by his mother —clad in a dressing-gown and followed by George. Without any hesitation George sat down on the couch and put his arm around Floria. Judy rose and, still rather fearful, she looked up at her husband. His face was a little grey, which was to be expected when someone had dropped dead in his house, but a smile touched his mouth and, reaching out, he took hold of Judy's hand and gave it a reassuring little squeeze.

It was two o'clock in the morning before Judy found herself alone with Chris. She had gone up to her room much earlier, for Chris had told both her and Floria to go to bed.

He himself had to see the doctor, who pronounced death to be caused from heart failure.

'Carried too much weight,' he had said in rather heartless tones. 'A young man like that should take more exercise. I make a practice of walking for at least an hour every day,' he went on, speaking to no one in particular. 'That's why I'm so fit at sixty-three years of age.'

Vincent had been taken to a little chapel of rest behind the harbour; George had at last gone, after having had a long talk with Chris when eventually they were alone. He had informed Chris earlier of his meetings with Floria, but later he told Chris that when a reasonably decent period of time had elapsed, he and Floria were to be married.

Chris repeated this to Judy when, having retired to his room, he realized the light was still on in hers. He tapped gently on the door and then opened it. Judy, in a pretty little frilly thing, was sitting on the bed, having just been in to Floria to see if she was all right. The girl couldn't sleep and Judy had suggested she either come in to her or go to her mother.

'I'll go to Mother,' Floria had said. 'I don't want to keep you awake all night, Judy.'

Judy did not mind in the least, but she felt that Floria would be better with her mother.

'You knew what was going on.' Chris made the statement after telling Judy about the conversation he had had with George. 'Why didn't you tell me?'

'One doesn't, Chris,' she returned simply. She knew there wouldn't be much to explain, for obviously George had left nothing unsaid, but Judy lifted her eyes, searching Chris's face, and then ventured hesitantly, 'How much did you overhear?'

'In the garden? Everything, I presume,' came the grim rejoinder. 'Although Corinne had obviously been speaking to you before you talked together in the garden.' Judy nodded and told him what Corinne had said about seeing her and George together, adding,

'She was talking about the "little escapade" as she called it, when you came up and interrupted. It's a wonder you didn't hear her.'

Chris did not seem to be taking that in, for after a preoccupied silence he said wrathfully,

'Why did you let me scare you like that?'

Her eyes opened very wide indeed.

'Scare?' she echoed, diverted. 'If that isn't an understatement I don't know what is! You had me petrified! I thought I'd have fainted, I was so terror-stricken!' Much to her disgust her husband's sole reaction to that was an amused curve of his lips. However, there was no amusement in his tones when he spoke. In fact they were both stern and censorious as he asked her why she hadn't defended herself.

'I know you were shielding Floria,' he added, 'but your position was desperate.'

So he did have the grace to admit that!

'I tried to get you to let me speak to Floria, if you remember,' she told him patiently, 'but you were in such a fury you wouldn't listen.' And, because she was now so sure of him, 'I don't know how you could believe such a thing of me! You ought to be ashamed of yourself!'

'I should——?' He stared down at her from a great height. 'Perhaps you'll tell me what the devil I was supposed to think after what I'd overheard!'

Judy thought about this and a rueful smile curved her mouth.

'I suppose it did sound damning,' she admitted. 'Yes, perhaps there's an excuse for your anger.'

'I saw red; jealousy blinded me to everything—to the obvious flaw in the whole thing, to the logic and to the trust, even.'

'Certainly you didn't trust me,' Judy was quick to agree, her eyes flashing indignantly.

'You can drop the self-righteous air,' was his cutting rejoinder. 'You didn't trust me, either.' Judy swallowed; she had forgotten he'd heard everything. Corinne had talked openly of her affair with Chris, saying Judy must turn a blind eye when he went away for week-ends. By her lack of response Judy had accepted the fact that an affair was going on.

'You'd been having an affair with Corinne,' she said in self-defence. 'So—so I did have an excuse for mistrusting you.' Watching him, Judy saw a movement at the side of his jaw; he said, meeting her gaze,

'You speak in the past tense, Judy.' And he paused a moment before he added, 'Do you believe I'm having an affair now?'

She flinched, but shook her head.

'No, I believe it's finished now.' He did not speak. She wished he would deny ever having had an affair with Corinne even while she knew he could not do so with truth. And she knew also that he would not lie to her. But as she searched his face she was satisfied. Corinne had never meant anything to him since his marriage, and she would never do so from now on. 'You,' she said at length, 'you didn't really believe that of me, Chris, did you?'

He moved close and took hold of both her hands.

'As I've said, darling, it was jealousy—and temper, of course. I was inflamed, but I should have stopped to think.' He smiled tenderly and tilted her face with a gentle hand under her chin. 'No, darling, I didn't think that of you—not deep down inside.'

Darling.... Her heart swelled as happiness flooded

over her. How could she have been so stupid as to think she had lost him?

'You called me that once before,' she murmured shyly, and Chris bent his head and kissed her, but he did not comment on her hesitantly uttered words and she went on to relate what Floria had said about her father's arrogance and his dominating attitude. 'I soon decided you'd been allowing me my own way because you had learned a lesson from the break-up of your parents' marriage.' Her words were a question and when he had explained she knew that once again her deductions had proved to be correct.

'I loved you on sight,' he then told her, drawing her close into his arms. 'But I must admit I meant to keep you in your place. However, I do possess my share of intelligence and the moment you began your little battles I remembered Mother. Then it was that I realized I could lose you, when you were older. And as I wanted you for always I began to tread warily.' He held her to him and kissed her passionately. 'I also knew I wanted you for my partner and my equal and not as a pretty little plaything.' He drew away, looked deeply into her eyes, and she saw that his own eyes held a hint of amusement. He was laughing at her again and she said,

'My little battles as you call them weren't really necessary—not after a while, were they?'

'They weren't, Judy, but it was a pleasant game and I thoroughly enjoyed it.'

She looked severely at him for a moment and then, not without a hint of puzzlement,

'Didn't you want me?' It was strange, but she did not feel at all shy—not even in the scanty attire she wore.

'Want you!' he ejaculated. 'My lovely wife—of course I wanted you!'

'Well, then...?' Judy *was* shy now, and she lowered

her head and then buried it in his coat. Chris laughed softly, raised her head and kissed one burning cheek, tenderly and lovingly.

'That first night, sweetheart, you were so scared and so young. I'd waited so long already—of necessity, of course—and I suddenly realized I could very easily create in you a revulsion for me, so I decided to wait a little while longer, especially as at that time there was the added complication of this Ronnie whom you thought you loved.'

'Thought?' She glanced up quickly. 'I did love him once——'

'Nonsense!' he interrupted, amused. 'Had you really loved him you'd have flatly refused to marry me. Neither I nor your grandfather could have forced you to marry me——' He broke off and a slight tremor passed through him. 'I might have seemed inflexible and overbearing, my dear, but I was afraid—terribly afraid I might lose you.'

Judy trembled then and clung to him tightly.

'I'm glad you were inflexible and overbearing—— Oh, Chris, wouldn't it have been awful if I'd married Ronnie!'

'I don't believe you would have married him. You'd have discovered your true feelings in time, discovered you didn't love him at all.'

'But I'd have lost you——' A kiss prevented her saying more, a kiss that was ardent and long. 'I'm sure now that I was beginning to like you,' she continued when he had released her and she had managed to get back her breath. 'That's why I made no protest. It must have been a subconscious thing.' She went up on tiptoe and kissed him, her eyes shining with love, and with something akin to adoration. 'Chris. . . .'

'Darling?'

'Did you think I would fall in love with you?'

'I hoped to make you love me, dearest; that's why I was so patient and why I regarded your struggles with such tolerance.'

'You exaggerated when you said I bullied you!' Chris laughed.

'So I did; I felt like pandering to your ego. You were obviously so delighted with your progress——'

'That was horrid of you!' she protested and again he laughed. But he said with mock severity,

'Stop looking like a termagant! I threatened once to beat you, so take care.' Despite this he pressed his lips to hers in a kiss that was both reverent and passionate, both gentle and possessive. 'Did you really want me to be a weak and submissive type of man—or was Ali Baba right when he said you weren't honest?' He held her away from him, his eyes alight with humour. Judy laughed and blushed and shook her head.

'Ali Baba was right,' she admitted, but went on to say with feigned anger and indignation that Chris was downright mean to enjoy himself at her expense.

'I knew you were laughing at me,' she ended, pouting.

'I couldn't help laughing, sweetheart. It was so diverting watching you fighting for freedom when in fact you were already free.'

'But you said yourself you meant to keep me in my place,' she reminded him, 'so I must have achieved something.' It was too much altogether to confess, even to herself, that all her struggles had been unnecessary.

'All right, darling, you did,' he admitted frankly. 'You brought back the memory of Mother's struggles, and of what resulted because of Father's obstinacy.'

A small silence followed and then, because she just had to know, Judy asked if Chris had accepted a dowry from her grandfather. But instantly she wished she hadn't, for a cold metallic gleam entered his eyes and his lips compressed.

'I had no need of a dowry,' he almost snapped.

Judy's lip quivered.

'I'm sorry, Chris, but I just had to ask.'

He became gentle, much to her relief.

'I've said I married you for love—that I loved you from the first moment of setting eyes on you. I also told you once that I offered for you because I didn't want anyone else to have the opportunity of doing so.' He spoke softly, a wealth of love and tenderness in his voice, and Judy wondered why she should have jumped to the conclusion that he had offered simply because of desire.

'Your phrasing was wrong,' she murmured, unaware that she spoke aloud until Chris asked her what she meant. 'When you said you offered because you were afraid someone else would do so I thought it was just—just...' She tailed off, her blushes telling him the rest.

'Just desire for your body?' He shook his head, rather sadly. 'You're a silly, puss, Judy,' he admonished. 'Why did you jump to all those stupid conclusions?' She merely nestled close, her head on his shoulder. But after a little while she voiced a question that had been puzzling her of late.

'Corinne ... were you trying to make me jealous?'

'I was,' he owned freely. 'It was becoming so hard to wait and I'm afraid I resorted to making an endeavour to arouse your jealousy in order to help you to see the light—to make you realize you loved me and desired me just as much as I desired you.'

Judy's head remained on his shoulder, for she would not let him see her expression, and after a few moments he told her that Corinne was leaving the island very soon. Judy did not pursue this subject, having a shrewd suspicion that Chris had tackled Corinne about what he had overheard in the garden, and then had given her a piece of his mind. However, Judy did look up after a while and her expression revealed all the relief she felt at the knowledge that his ex-girl-friend was leaving Hydra. She felt sure Corinne would never return.

'My dear, dear love.' Chris spoke softly, yet with a vibrancy that thrilled and excited her, and she lifted her face for his kiss. He was infinitely tender and gentle, yet there was a possessive quality in the warmth and strength of his body, so very close to hers. She quivered under the touch of his hands, feeling their warmth through the thinness of her attire, and as the silent moments passed she became profoundly aware of his rising ardour and the heavy uneven thudding of his heart above her own. Judy could not speak ... but her response to his kiss told him all he wanted to know.

Mills & Boon
Best Seller Romances

The very best of Mills & Boon
brought back for those of you
who missed reading them when they
were first published.
There are three other Best Seller Romances
for you to collect this month.

THE GARDEN OF DREAMS
by Sara Craven

Lissa wasn't quite sure whether or not she really wanted to marry
the attractive Frenchman Paul de Gue, so she was glad to accept his
invitation to visit the family château and meet his relatives.
Unfortunately this also involved meeting the austere Comte Raoul de
Gue – who made it clear that he did *not* want Lissa marrying into
the family!

VALLEY OF THE VAPOURS
by Janet Dailey

If Tisha didn't get away from her domineering father soon, he and she
were going to come to blows! So she went off to spend a long holiday
with her sympathetic Aunt Blanche – and met Roarke Madison, who
was even fonder of telling her what to do than her father had been!

THE BEACH OF SWEET RETURNS
by Margery Hilton

The little beach had been Kate's childhood paradise. But she returned
home to Malaya, a successful model, determined to make no
sentimental pilgrimages. For ever since her first unhappy love affair
Kate wore the cool assurance of her career as a defence she vowed no
man would ever break down. But she reckoned without
Brad Sheridan . . .

If you have difficulty in obtaining any of these books through
your local paperback retailer, write to:

Mills & Boon Reader Service
P.O. Box 236, Thornton Road, Croydon, Surrey, CR9 3RU

How to join in a whole new world of romance

It's very easy to subscribe to the Mills & Boon Reader Service. As a regular reader, you can enjoy a whole range of special benefits. Bargain offers. Big cash savings. Your own free Reader Service newsletter, packed with knitting patterns, recipes, competitions, and exclusive book offers.

We send you the very latest titles each month, postage and packing free – no hidden extra charges. There's absolutely no commitment – you receive books for only as long as you want.

We'll send you details. Simply send the coupon – or drop us a line for details about the Mills & Boon Reader Service Subscription Scheme.
Post to: Mills & Boon Reader Service, P.O. Box 236, Thornton Road, Croydon, Surrey CR9 3RU, England.
*Please note: READERS IN SOUTH AFRICA please write to: Mills & Boon Reader Service of Southern Africa, Private Bag X3010, Randburg 2125, S. Africa.

Please send me details of the Mills & Boon Subscription Scheme.
NAME (Mrs/Miss) _____ EP3
ADDRESS _____
_____

COUNTY/COUNTRY_____ POST/ZIP CODE_____
BLOCK LETTERS, PLEASE

Mills & Boon
the rose of romance